Olúróunbí's Promise,

AN AFrican FoLKtaLe

Princess Sherifat Akóredé

Illustrated by

Súnkànmí Akínbóyè

Olúróunbí's Promise, An African Folktale
Copyright © 2018 by Princess Sherifat Akóredé / Royal
Heritage Publishing Company

5

Princess Sherifat Akóredé

CONTENTS

REVIEWS

Olurounbi's Promise is a unique glimpse into the Nigerian town of Yorubaland, where typical experiences of West African life coalesce with compelling mysticism to form valuable lessons. Princess Sherifat reminds us of the power of storytelling and the value of discovering cultures different from our own.

Alex Melone
(TypeRight Editing)

As an adolescent, I fondly remember Princess Sherifat gathering my relatives and I for "story time." Her narration immersed us in elaborate worlds far beyond our native Chicago upbringing, yet we saw ourselves in the stories and grew a deep affinity for the characters. I am thrilled to have these stories take new life in her first book so I can share them with the next generation of young people, as they develop their spirituality, family values, and empathy towards others.

Ahrif Sarumi
(Founder of Aces of Taste, Houston)

"I enjoyed it as much as the children of Lagos. I loved the nuanced and details that show the reader what it's like to live in Lagos. You enrich your story with that care and attention to specifics that makes you story even more interesting to someone that has never traveled to Africa. The details like the types of food being cooked or not sitting under the tree bring your story to life. I also liked the delicate and precise characterization of your primary and secondary characters. The couple is loving and realistic, and the in-laws are even more realistic in their different approaches to family problems. Excellent work."

Alex Perry
(Houston Writers Guild, Texas).

"Get ready to be enchanted by a warm, funny, sad, and loving story set in Africa. When Olurounbi's and her husband had not given birth to a child soon after their marriage, some people started insulting and blaming them for it. Their love for each other and their faith kept them together. Princess Sherifat takes you on a journey among the Yoruba people of Nigeria that you never want to come to an end."

Aisha Ọsányìn,
La Reve Bridal Couture

The uniqueness of this story lies in the fact that *Ìrókò* tree, displaying ambivalent characteristics is not a true antagonist. It's dimensionality results in a very interesting outcome."

Muhibat   *Edunjobi*
University of Illinois (Chicago)

Hmmm, imagery, descriptive and colorful language!
    You were able to immerse your readers in the rich culture, as well as juxtapose a love story.

If anyone wants to initiate a Romance with West African culture, they can start by reading "Olurounbi's Promise".

You did justice to the gift of being a committed author...you took your readers on a journey.

Latifat Saaka
English Teacher, Houston Independent School
District (HISD)

ÀFIHÀN - INTRODUCTION

From birth until the age of sixteen, I lived in Lagos, Nigeria. Having only traveled overseas once on the Holy Pilgrimage to Saudi Arabia. My time in Nigeria was either spent going on trips to Abẹòkúta, Ògùn State with my maternal grandmother for the annual Muslim Eid Festival or to Ògbómọshọ, Ọyọ State for occasional visits to see my paternal grandfather.

At the age of seventeen, I moved to the Middle East which was a highly transformative experience. I sojourned there with my father who was a Nigerian diplomat, along with the rest of the family for the next four years. During this period of my life, I was exposed to Yorùbá folktales, Arabian tales, and English fairy tales, primarily from my grandparents, my older sister, Alhaja Ganiat Akóredé, and my father, Chief Imam Sheikh Prince Muritala (Murtadha) Àkànbí Akóredé, an admired story-teller and lyric composer in both English and Yorùbá Language. My father transferred much of his tales and oral tradition skills to his children, relatives, wards, and so many others who encountered him. Hence, my love for storytelling and knack for the embellishment of the originals.

When I relocated to the United States at the end of the 1980s decade, I shared many of the Yorùbá folklore and Islamic/Arabian tales of my youth to my children, relatives, and friends.

Being an avid reader from a family of readers, helped in expanding my knowledge base and in igniting my love for writing which has finally manifested itself into this novel. Olúróunbí's Promise is meant to be a cultural and spiritual but secular book that adherents of any religion or belief can comfortably relate to. Spirituality is a vital and integral part of the Yorùbá people's lives, irrespective of the religion they follow. They believe in a supreme being that everything and everyone ultimately defers to, hence the word God is used as a representative of that supreme being.

As a parent and a relatively new grandparent, I realize that it is very important to join others in leaving a legacy of transmitting and sharing African (Yorùbá) folklore with the general world population in written and oral form. With the rise in popularity of Pro-Black and African films, music, and art; I consider this period to be a neo-renaissance of African pride in America which celebrates, not conceals our identities.

Regarding the Yorùbá language, many are concerned that it is endangered and may become extinct in less than a century. Although it is spoken in the southwestern region of Nigeria, The Republic of Benin, Togo, pockets of communities in the United Kingdom and the United States of America; and has recently been declared an official language in Brazil, it is being replaced with English in Nigerian homes. Its use is banned and forbidden in many households and schools. Yoruba is classified by some as "vernacular" and thus seen as inferior to English. Many individuals view the speaking of English as a sign of affluence and modernization. English is also the official language in Nigeria as it is in many other countries colonized by the British. Consequently, people are not motivated to master their traditional languages, such as Yoruba. Although I am not a master of Yoruba language and culture, I like to align myself with the propagators of Yorùbá pride awakening. I hope the new generations will aid in righting the wrong that has been done and take pride in their heritage.

I am very happy that my goal to contribute is taking shape and will come to fruition, by God's Grace. I hope you will enjoy the journey with Olúróunbí and her promise to Ìrókò tree, King of the woods.

Ọ̀RỌ̀ ÌṢÁÁJÚ - FOREWORD

After many, many years of writing, Olúróunbí's Promise is finally a reality. The author, who also happens to be my mother, spent several years compiling the chapters that make up this story. It grew and transformed many times before it took its final form, a first of a series. Olúróunbí's Promise is a story that merges African folklore with a modern perspective.

It is also a story that has pulled me in many times during the editing process. Despite having heard the original folktale many times in the duration of my childhood, I am simultaneously surprised and proud of what my mother has turned it into. If you are a Nigerian, you will appreciate this take on the original lore. If you aren't, you will learn a whole lot about the culture. Either way, I invite you to jump in. Thanks for reading!

Rashidat Ọmọlọlá Ẹdúnjọbí

December 2018

Ọ̀RỌ̀ ÀKỌ́SỌ - PREFACE

This project was born out of the realization that most Nigerian children both in the homeland and in the Diaspora did not know Yorùbá stories. They romanced English/Western tales. As a parent, I was part of the problem. I invested a lot of money in collecting the Cinderella, Snow White, Barbie, Ken, Aladdin, Jasmine, Rapunzel, Shrek, Mulan, books, music, and movies to list a few. My daughters even competed on their favorite characters. *Hmm ...* and we wonder why children of immigrant parents in the western world have an identity crisis.

In retrospect, I realize that I have always admired the richness of African culture, tradition, dressing, history, lifestyle, and food as I was always drawn to books and stories from all parts of African, in addition to my immersion western literature.

In the middle of working on an adult novel manuscript, I decided to suspend it and I started writing a collection of seven Yorùbá children's tales with Ìjàpá (the trickster and mischievous tortoise) as the central character. The stories of Ìjàpá were every child's favorite. After completing four or five of the manuscript, something persistently nagged me to publish Olúróunbí's story first. Ever since I was an adolescent, the story of Olúróunbí having sacrificed her daughter was always harrowing my mind. I pondered on why a parent would opt to give her daughter as a sacrifice in exchange for material things. So, I decided to publish the story of Olúróunbí first.

The completed manuscript was 32 pages of text. In order to provide a visual aid for the targeted age range, I started the tedious task of getting a Yorùbá artist who could give the illustration the authenticity that I desire. Then, I started sharing the manuscript with my critique group at the Houston Writers Guild. It literally opened a can of nice worms. They demanded more contextual, setting, cultural, and language information. Ms. Asi Williams and Ms., Muhibat Ẹdúnjọbí were the first to point out that some of the themes were not appropriate for the audience intended; yet they were peculiar societal issues that needed to be brought to light. Thus, I embarked on the rewrite process of Olúróunbí's Promise. At the end of the day, it turned out to almost quadruple length. The project transformed from a 38-page children's storybook to almost two hundred pages of young adult (YA) novel. It was a fantastically stressful and exciting journey. I love it!

The story consists of plots and subplots, themes and sub-themes that stretches over multiple generations that would incidentally bring to life a she-hero (Olúfúnmi, daughter of Olúróunbí) of uncommon power, qualities, and character that young people can relate to. Her heroism will be demonstrated in how she surmounts extremely powerful negative forces and formidable enemies among humans, jinns, animals and supernatural creatures.

Several months of writing, proofreading, editing, rewriting and re-editing, the manuscript was completed with all the Yorùbá names and words still in the Latin script. I wanted the book to be as authentic as possible. Also, part of my aim is to provide the opportunity for non-Yorùbá speakers to use it as a tool to learn some Yorùbá names, words, and phrases. I hope you can benefit from this effort.

Thank you and Be Blessed.

Chapter One
ÈKÓ – Lagos, Nigeria
1975

"Ugh, NEPA!" echoed across the densely populated city of Lagos. Blackness enveloped the houses and the streets. Even the streetlights went out, but instead of dampened spirits and anger, the youngsters from each family started giggling and laughing. The Nigerian National Electric Power Authority (NEPA) had wielded its authority, as usual, to eliminate light from parts of Lagos City. No one knew how long the outage would last.

After helping her mother lit a wax candle, Làbáké rushed to the corner of the room where the straw mats rested against the wall. She grabbed one and ran out of her family's two-room apartment, her farewell, "*Ódàbọ̀, màámi,*" trailing behind her. *Màmá* Làbáké smiled, shaking her head. I wonder which tale Alhaji Ọlómọwéwé will narrate today.

Làbáké almost collided with a couple of boys who were racing each other to the coconut palm tree in the middle of the Àyìnké Housing courtyard. Even though she couldn't catch up, she joined in the race. Children from several houses spilled onto the streets and were assembling in varying clusters, some carrying lanterns, others armed with battery-operated torch lights, and some without anything to light their way. Several children were already buzzing like bees on their woven mats made of straw and rubber. All parents knew that their children belonged to Alhaji during power-outages. The only children who did not get to attend the storytelling under the palm tree were those who were sick or grounded by their parents.

Làbáké rolled out her mat as closely as she could to the base of the tree where Alhaji usually sat. The world's best storyteller liked to sit on a mat and rest his back against the tree's trunk.

This time, the power outage occurred just as the Muslim call to prayer rang through the streets. The call, signaling full sunset, was heard over loudspeakers from the surrounding Mosques just as families prepared for supper and other end-of-day activities. Alhaji emerged from the small

Mosque in the compound, beaming from ear to ear. His eyes danced over his children—he called all the neighborhood children his. He didn't treat his own four biological children and his three nephews and niece who lived with him with any preference. He was adored by all the children and most of the adults in the area.

A commotion erupted when the assembled children sighted Alhaji Ọlọ́mọwẹ́wẹ́ emerging from the Mosque. The Muslim children who were among the congregation trailed behind him respectfully, despite their eagerness. As soon as Alhaji moved out of the way, the children behind him raced to the mats and squeezed into the dwindling open spaces.

"Daddy!" The children said in unison, giving him the patriarchal title as a sign of respect. "Good evening, sir." The boys prostrated and the girls took to both knees.

"*Eká alẹ́, gbogbo ẹ̀yin ọmọ mi* (Good evening, my children)." He waved at his expectant audience. "So, you have begged NEPA to switch off the power tonight, so you can have an excuse to come and listen to stories, *hennn, Àbí?*"

"Noooo! We did not, sir ooo!" they chorused.

"But we are glad they took the power, sir," offered a girl of about eleven years old. "If not, our parents wouldn't have allowed us to come out tonight. You are the only one they allow us to come together in the evening for, sir."

"Okay," he smiled, lowering his body onto the outer-grown root at the foot of the tree. He nodded greetings at his closest friend, Pastor James, who had already taken a seat alongside the other adults. He smiled and returned the nod. Alhaji and Pastor James were childhood friends from their grade school days. Their fathers had worked together at the Nigerian Railway Corporation during the British colonial rule in Nigeria. They lived in the same neighborhood of Àpápá Road, Èbúté-Mẹta. Their wives also became the best of friends, and they looked out for each other's children. As a result, their combined ten children became close. The two families celebrated the Muslim Eid festivals and the Christian holidays harmoniously. Pastor James never missed his friend's storytelling if he was around. His house was situated on a parallel street behind Alhaji's house. The pastor's seven children were also in attendance of their favorite pastime during the power outage.

The assembled younger children crouched near his chair, even though they knew that they would be redirected.

"My children, you know the rules, don't you?"

"Yes, sir." Their sullen voices were accompanied by their instantaneous obedience. Feet scraped the ground as the children inched backward. Alhaji Olómowéwé always insisted that they sat outside the brush of the tree to avoid coconut-inflicted head injuries. An impressive number of young men and adults had also assembled behind the children, each having brought his folding chair along. Alhaji observed that none of the few women who usually partook in the storytelling were present. He guessed that they must be busy with house chores, cooking supper and taking care of the family, as usual.

After a satisfactory safety inspection of the children and ensuring that he was seated close enough to the tree trunk where coconuts could not stray, Alhaji cleared his throat playfully. He nodded at the two boys, Gabriel and Abdul-Salaam, cradling *gángan talking drums* under one arm and holding the sticks with the opposing hand. Signaling the commencement of the storytelling event, they started beating the *gángan talking drums*, gifted to them by the neighborhood *Àyàn* (professional drummer). The children responded with bobbing heads, shoulders, and flailing arms and hands in rhythm to the familiar melody. Alhaji signaled, and the drumming stopped. He started.

"*Ààló ̣ooo* (Storytime)."

"*Ààló ̣!*" The crowd replied in unison with the drums.

Alhaji stretched the sound like an elastic band.

"*Ààààló ̣!*" The audience and the drums, following Alhaji's cue, replied louder and longer. Young giggles and deeper chuckles accompanied the response backed by a series of drumbeats.

"*Àààààààlọ́ ooo*," he elongated it further, enjoying the impatience of the little ones, whose eyes were nearly popping out of their sockets.

"*Àààààààààlọ!*" The children surrendered to wild excitement, knowing that the suspense was over, and their adventure was beginning. The drums infused the air with thrill.

"*Ní ìgbà kan* (Once upon a time) ...."

"*Ìgbà kan ń lọ; ìgbà kan ń bọ̀; ọjọ́ ń gorí ọjọ́* (Time goes; time comes; day overtakes another day)." The audience recited the familiar response.

"Thousands of lunar months ago..." Alhaji paused for effect. His amused eyes once again danced over the listeners. He smiled, basking in their full attention. He rested his gaze longer on the usually fidgety seven-year-old Kúnlé, who had been nicknamed *Ara-ò-balẹ̀* because of his hyperactivity and inattentive disposition. Alhaji smiled at Kúnlé and gave him an approving nod. Kúnlé returned an ear-to-ear grin and remained as calm as *omi àmù,* water stored overnight in a large clay water vessel, and as attentive as the elderly village mediator.

"And many, *many* tortoise generations ago…"

Làbáké, as usual, raised her hand, requesting permission to speak. Alhaji gave a knowing smile, looked at her, and glanced at the pastor. They exchanged smiles, thinking, *we know she's going to ask questions for sure.* Alhaji signaled to Làbáké to proceed.

She stood up, respectfully placed her hands behind her back, and cleared her throat importantly. "Daddy, sir, why do you always say 'Many, *many* tortoise generations ago,' sir? We all know that each lunar month is twenty-nine or thirty days and one thousand months equals eighty-three years. But we don't know how long a tortoise's life, or their generation is."

"Good question, Làbáké."

Làbáké grinned happily and curtsied at Alhaji; she glared *òọ́bì* at a couple of boys who had accused her of interrupting the storytelling to get attention. They glared their *òọ́bì* back at her as she sat down on the mat. "You just want people to think you're smarter than everybody else, right?"

They often complained. "That's not true!" Làbáké retorted.

The feudal exchange between the boys and Làbáké didn't go unnoticed. "Thank you, Làbáké; no question is a stupid question. It gives everyone the opportunity to gain deeper knowledge on a subject. Well, we say that because tortoises are among the animals that live for a long time. Many of them live longer than a hundred years if not killed. By the way, do you know that the longest living tortoise in the world right now lives in Nigeria?"

Several eyebrows were raised. "Really?" Many voices responded. "Where in Nigeria? Lagos? Ìbàdàn zoo? The north?"

"Really! Yes, in this very country of yours."

"Which State and City, sir? Please, please, sir. Tell us, sir," pleaded the younger children.

"In Ọyọ State!" Alhaji announced brightly. Those whose native hometowns were in Ọyọ State broke in loud cheers while the rest of the children made a pseudo-disappointed sound.

"What part of Ọyọ State?" they wanted to know.

Alhaji glanced at his friend who was beaming. "It is not living in a zoo. This tortoise is considered royalty because it lives in the palace of Ọba Ṣọ̀ún of Ògbómọ̀shọ́. It has been living there for about three hundred years. History tells us that it was brought into Ṣọ̀ún's Palace in the 1770s by the third king who resigned after the kingdom of Ògbómọ̀shọ́ was founded, Ọba Ikúmóyèdé Àjàó."

Suddenly, the audience heard another voice interrupt Alhaji, and their heads turned in its direction. "Can you, children guess whose native hometown is Ògbómọ̀shọ́?" It was unmistakably the familiar voice of the pastor.

Following the rules of storytelling participation, several hands flew up, including Alhaji's and the pastor's children. "I know, I know," several voices shouted.

Alhaji's lips spread from eastern ear to the western one, lifting his high cheekbones into two oblong buns on his face. The pastor pointed his index finger at a child that did not belong to his household nor Alhaji's. He picked a boy who lived at least a seven minutes' sprint from Alhaji's residence. "Tell us!"

"You, sir," he replied tentatively, pointing at the pastor.

"No. I am not from Ògbómọ̀shọ́. I'm from Ìbàdàn. I know your guess is because of the tribal marks on my face." A broad smile spread across the pastor's face. "It is my good friend here," he pointed at Alhaji. The children who knew Alhaji's hometown nodded while those who did not know made an "ah!" surprised sound.

"Thank you, my dear pastor. Yes, indeed my father is from the Láoyè Dynasty, which is one of the ruling houses in Ògbómọ̀shọ́. Like I said earlier, the tortoise Alàgbà has been part of the palace household for almost three centuries."

Làbákẹ́ raised her hand again but was too eager to wait for permission to speak to be granted. She asked, "So, why do tortoises live for such a long time?"

"That's a story for another day, Làbákẹ́. You know I have told you so many stories of Ìjàpá the tortoise, right?"

"*Bẹ́ẹ̀ni sà!* Yes, sir!" chorused the children.

"One day, I will tell you all about Alàgbà, all right?"

The drummers signaled the end of the digression with a series of talking drums, instructing the continuation of Olúróunbí.

Alhaji, who was nearing fifty years old, couldn't resist the calling of the drum; he effortlessly sprang to his feet. His shoulders began to jump up and down, curving and rolling in rhythm with the dictates of the *gángan*. His jacquard *agbádá, bùbá* àti *sòkòtò (*three-piece *Yorùbá men's flowy garment)* rustled and whirled by the power unleashed from every joint of his arms. Most of the children jumped to their feet and joined Alhaji in the *baata* dance. He danced with the virility and agility of a twenty-year-old man.

Alhaji Ọlómọwẹ́wẹ́, a soccer and ping-pong table tennis player in his younger days, looked thirtyish. There was no visible fat on any part of his body. Even though he no longer played soccer, he played table tennis several days a week and often beat most of his opponents at the commercial table tennis spot across the street from his house. Whenever a player from other neighborhoods came and won every set of the game, the neighborhood youths would go and complain to him.

"Daddy! There's a boy from another neighborhood who had put our 'area' champions to shame. He beat all our best players mercilessly!" they would report with indignation.

"Who is the boy? How could you allow someone from anywhere to come here and beat us?"

"Our boys tried seriously *ooo*, sir, but this man was good, fast, and ruthless. He beat every challenger."

"Well, then invite him over next weekend and we'll see how good and fast he is." The conversation with the neighborhood emissary usually ended on that note. The ping-pong table tennis champion would come over to Alhaji's "area," engage in a fierce game of several sets, and Alhaji would win without much sweat. Most of Alhaji's efforts were centered on his wrist and his long arms. He hardly ever ran helter-skelter after the tiny egg. His opponents usually did the running around. His good-natured smile rarely ever left his face. He remained the undefeated champion until one day when he was defeated by his own sixteen-year-old son, Ìyàndá. It was a historic day in the neighborhood—and beyond. The news seemed to have traveled at the speed of a raging forest fire when Ìyàndá won two of the three sets of the game. Spectators surrounding the players blocked the roadway. Other spectators of all ages and gender lined up on the balconies and terraces overlooking the street. Ìyàndá had mastered his father's style and techniques. Neither of them sweated, however, Ìyàndá's youthfulness gave him a slight advantage over his father. It was a Saturday, and neither father nor son was willing to be the first to call for an end to the game. Eventually, after several hours of playing, the owner of the ping-pong table called for the end of the game. At that time, the game stats were 7 to 3 sets of three in favor of Ìyàndá. He approached his father and lowered his entire body to the ground in prostration and congratulated his father for what he called the greatest game of his life. Alhaji placed his hand on his son's head lovingly, then pulled him up to a standing position and pronounced him the new champion of Èbúté-Mẹ́ta causing wild cheers and applause to erupt from the crowd.

Alhaji's firm lanky body surprisingly moved like a professional dancer just as it did at the ping-pong game with ease. The children, having scattered the mats on the ground with their frenzy dancing, rearranged and settled back on the mats as soon as the drum roll combination signaled the end of the round.

During the story time, Ìyàndá sat beside his fifteen-year-old friend, son of Pastor James.

Back on his chair, Alhaji continued with the story. *"Ìyàwó àti ọkọ kan wa.* (There existed a woman and her husband)." He heard the unmistakable squeaky anticipatory excitement of the young children as he introduced the characters of the day's story. He knew their individual minds were wondering if it was a story they had heard before or a new one. Although the adults were calmer, they did not try to hide the pleasure readable on their faces.

"Wọ́n wà bí ẹ̀wà (They exist as beans exist)."
The young drummers showed off their prowess in enunciating each syllable in sync with the audience.

"Ààlọ́ mi leri, o leri, o leri isele kan ni ilu kan nile Yorùbá. (My story is about an event that occurred in the town of Yorùbá land)."

"Sorry, sir. We forgot." Their sullen voices did not mirror their instant obedience. They inched back, measuring the peripheral range of an incidental fall of a ripe coconut on their heads again. Satisfied, Alhaji continued with the tale. The younger children crouched closer to Alhaji's chair again. They seemed to have forgotten the instructions. "My children, what rules are you breaking again?" he asked them.

37

Chapter Two
LẸ́HÌN ÌGBÉYÀWÓ – AFTER THE WEDDING

The couple had been married for three years without bearing a child. The name of the bride was Olúróunbí Ọdẹ́táyé, the groom Ayọ̀ Àjàní. In their homeland called Ìlúgidi, it was unacceptable for a young couple not to have a child within the first year of marriage. The families of both Olúróunbí and Ayọ̀ became increasingly worried. "Why haven't you brought a baby into the world yet?" They were often asked. Some of the town folks even taunted them, and enviously gossiped about their closeness. "How can Olúróunbí and Ayọ̀ continue pretending to be happy when they can't even have babies all this time that they've been married?" Others would express annoyance when they were seen holding hands or chatting cheerfully under their favorite guava tree nearby. Their own parents even declared that they were hiding their faces in shame because of the town's gossip.

"Don't you want to make us happy with grandchildren in our old age—before we pass on?" Mama Ayọ̀ asked many times.

"Ayọ̀! Olúróunbí! Let us know what the problem is so that we know what to do about it," Olúróunbí's mother pleaded.

Each time Ayọ̀ and Olúróunbí replied, "Màmá, you know that children are gifts from The One who created us all. He will give us our children at His time." During a visit by both parents, Ayọ̀ turned to face his parents squarely. "You have to ignore the town's gossip and nonsense talk," he admonished. "We all just need to be steadfast in our prayers and kindness to others, and our wishes will be granted." He said with a firm finality in his voice. Ayọ̀ attempted to change the topic to a more cheerful current event but before he could speak, his father sprang swiftly from the straw-filled sheep wool *tim-tim* seat and stood upright in front of his son, almost touching his nose. Bàbá Ayọ̀, a tall man, was proud that his son was taller and more intelligent than him, even though he seldom showed it. He considered it the fulfillment of God's benevolence for his offspring to be greater than him as his people commonly prayed for. He was about to make some utterance, when Màmá Ayọ̀ scrambled to her feet just in time to lay her hand gently on his, the meaning of which he immediately understood. He swallowed hard, glanced at his wife, rearranged his facial affect, and forced a grin at Ayọ̀ and Olúróunbí. He recognized the promise of Heaven in those darling eyes of his wife if he obeyed her unspoken commands. "Yes, yes, yes—okay, my son. That is what we must persist in," he stated instead. Ayọ̀ could hear Olúróunbí's concealed sigh of relief.

"Well, we better take our leave now. It's almost sunset. It's a good time to pray to Our Creator to grant us our hearts' desires." Bàbá Ayọ̀ had come to terms a long time ago that he had no chance of going against his wife's advice. *She knows how to stroke my ego into believing that I'm the captain of this household ship.* No one discerned his secret smile as he recalled the times that his wife had pampered him in the privacy of their inner chambers. He almost lost the chance to have his feet soaked in a warm, powerful herbal solution and served *ẹ̀fọ́ rírò* greens garnished with an assortment of sun-dried fish, smoked hen, stir-fried snail, and other ingredients he could not name. Afterward, Heaven's gate would be thrown open for him underneath the blanket of the night. Ayọ̀ was grateful for his mother's intervention, and Olúróunbí marveled at the magical power in her mother-in-law. *The power of love!* She mused. *I hope I will attain Màmá Ayọ̀'s skills in managing Bàbá Ayọ̀'s temperament. Not that my darling has his father's volcanic temper, thank God! But every wife needs to be able to manage her husband like that.*

One day, when Olúróunbí was returning from a nearby market, she heard snickering and taunting from the townspeople. They called her names that did not belong to her, like "an empty barrel of a woman." Olúróunbí walked into their home with her face all wet and scrunched up. When Ayọ̀ greeted her, he noticed the tears streaming down her face. He quickly put his arms around her, sat her down on the bed, and asked, "Why are you crying, my love? What happened?" The alarm in his voice made her wipe her eyes quickly.

"Oh, my dear, it's nothing serious. I am probably just moody because it's that time of the month, you know." She forced a smile and a wink.

Ayọ̀ did not buy it because his wife did not cry easily. She was a strong woman, and Ayọ̀ knew it had to be something serious. He pressed further until Olúróunbí told him of how some people were throwing hurtful words at her as she walked home from the market. Ayọ̀ pulled his wife closer, draping his arm around her shoulders, wiped her face with his other hand, and flashed his big smile that never failed to comfort and reassure her of his love. She smiled. *He always knows how to console me.*

"Ọlọ́run (God) will soon bless us with our beautiful daughter who will look just like you or a handsome son who will be my carbon copy. Don't worry my love, soon the whole world will see! And the mouths of those mean people will be zipped up," Ayọ̀ assured his wife.

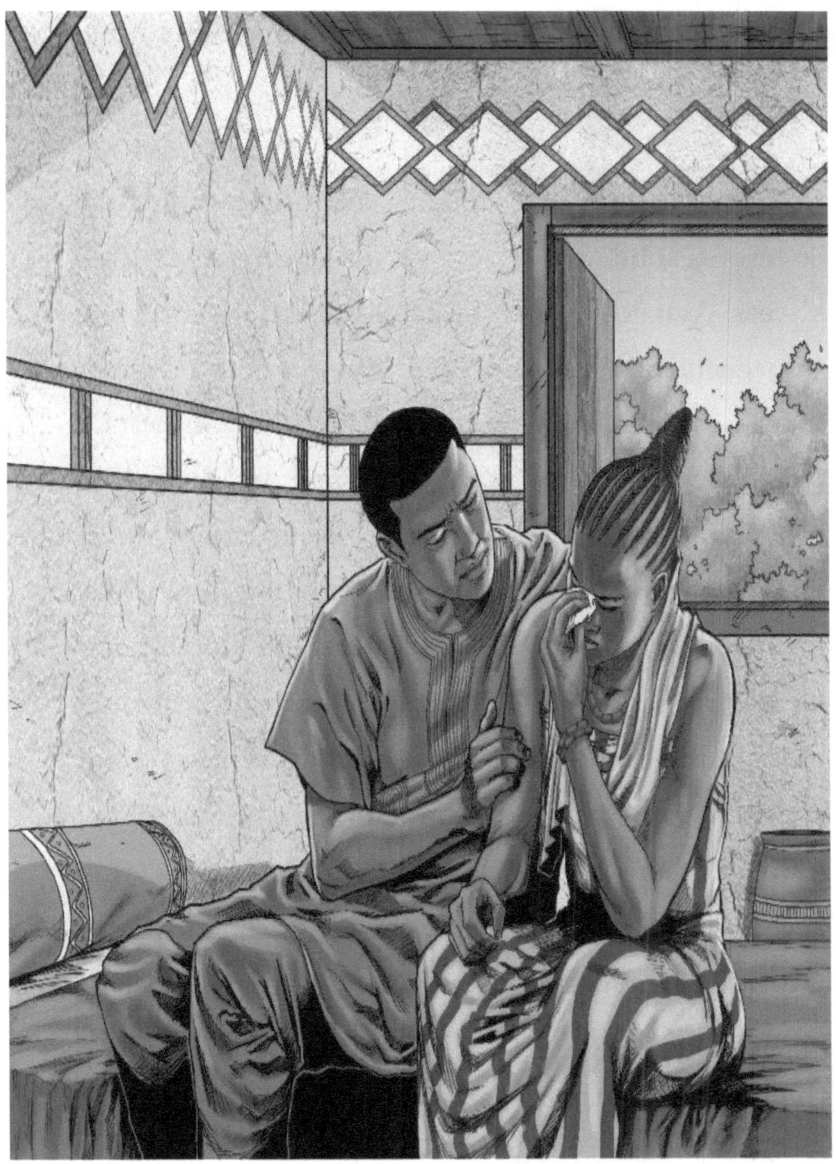

Olúróunbí chuckled, and Ayọ̀ joined in the laughter. If anyone had been nearby their small compound, they would have heard laughing through the walls.

Olúróunbí and Ayọ̀ lived in a single floor edifice constructed with limestone rocks, manually mixed concrete, solid woods and strips of iron rods and sheets. Ayọ̀ designed it himself with input from his fiancée at the time, Olúróunbí. Ayọ̀, who was living in the renovated ancient Àjàní family compound, purchased the piece of land as soon as Olúróunbí accepted his courtship on a probationary term after several months of pursuit. She had given him a tough time in order to ascertain his worthiness as her husband. She wanted a kind and strong man who possessed the right qualities and character. She refused to be seen with him until he had proven himself. Immediately after the acceptance of marriage and the conclusion of their family introduction ceremony, Ayọ̀ had the foundation of the structure laid and commenced the building of their matrimonial home.

They decided on a three-bedroom, a large parlor, a detached kitchen to the right of the building, and two detached toilets. The two bathrooms were constructed at the far end of the backyard. Ivory was the primary color selected for the exterior, and an artistic orange diamond overlay complemented the pillars and the footage of the house. The intricate brown painted border ran around the top part of the edifice, contrasting the ivory.

The couple's bedroom had a large window overlooking a botanical garden. The other two rooms were prepared for children and possible occasional guests. They both agreed that there was enough land to expand as the family increased in size.

One day, Ayọ̀ returned from his farm early and met his wife cooking in the compound. *"Ọkọ mi, Kàábọ̀ (Welcome! my husband)."* Olúróunbí courtesy slightly, bending her knees, a gesture that Ayọ̀ found both respectful and somewhat seductive. The way she rolled her hips while placing one hand on top of the other above her right knee sent shivers up and down his body. Ayọ̀ was not sure whether the style of greeting was to balance her gait or to allow the rolling of her hips and the projection of her chest toward him. All he knew was that he loved it, and it made him love and honor her more.

Ayọ̀ whispered into her ear, and they collapsed into each other's arms. Ayọ̀ held his wife close and allowed Olúróunbí to rest her head on his chest for as long as she wanted to. She seemed to be checking to make sure the pounding of his heart maintained the same strong rhythm as always. When she was satisfied, she proceeded with the usual, "Welcome, my love. How was your day? I hope work wasn't too tedious. Are you still on target for harvest?" All Ayọ̀'s responses were affirmative. After that, Ayọ̀ was informed that his bath water was waiting for him in the bathhouse. Ayọ̀ thanked Olúróunbí as he walked to the bathhouse at the backyard. Olúróunbí hurried to the kitchen. Ayọ̀ followed her until she veered left toward the kitchen, inhaling her sweet, intoxicating scents. Olúróunbí enjoyed cooking in the outdoors, except when it rained. She returned with a lidded pot filled with chopped okra she had cooked earlier and placed it beside other kitchen wares near the *àdògán (small* charcoal grill stove). She opened the steaming pot and transferred pieces of yam into a mortar. After a short while, she covered the pot so that the yam would continue being steamed. Olúróunbí, with significant effort, picked up the wooden pestle and commenced pounding the blemish-free white yam mercilessly inside the mortar. She added more pieces of yam from the steaming pot and raised the pestle several inches above the crown of her head and brought it down with determined might. Olúróunbí's arms, ribs, and back grunted, but her countenance painted a picture of pride. *I'm going to make the smoothest yam fufu swallow for my darling this evening.*

"Let me do it. Give me the *ọmọrí odó (pestle).* You go and finish up with the stew on the *àdògán* (small charcoal grill) and reduce the firewood under this pot of yam," Ayọ̀ commanded, taking the pestle with one hand, and steering Olúróunbí away from the mortar with the other hand. He had struggled to keep his ribs from bursting with stifled laughter as he had watched his wife fight a losing battle with the mortar, the pestle, and the hot yam.

Olúróunbí did not see Ayọ̀ emerge from the building; nor did she hear his footstep behind her. Therefore, she was slightly startled and embarrassed. "I can do it, Ayọ̀. Please, leave the *ọmọrí odó (pestle)!*"

"Of course, I know you can do it." He feigned a serious expression. "I just want to help you this time." He pleaded as he gave her a gentle push towards the coal-pot stove a few feet away.

Chapter Three

ÌPÀDÉ ÀWỌN ÒBÍ – MEETING OF THE PARENTS

Ayọ̀'s parents had invited Olúróunbí's parents to a family meeting at Ayọ̀ and Olúróunbí's house without notifying the hosts. Ayo's parents were the first to arrive.

Olúróunbí ran across the small single-family compound and went down on her knees, taking her mother-in-law's handbag in a single swift motion. *"Ha! Ẹkáàbò mà, ẹkáàbò sir,* (welcome)" she greeted them, showing gleaming white teeth, even though her chest pounded fast and loud like the pounding of the *yam* by Ayọ̀ earlier in the week. *"Ẹmáá wolẹ̀, ẹmáá rọra"* Olúróunbí continued to repeat like a parrot's regurgitation till they entered the house.

Màmá Ayọ̀ returned the smile and greetings with warmth, while Bàbá Ayọ̀ stabbed Olúróunbí with a fiery glare. "Is my son home?" he demanded, strutting majestically toward the plushiest velvet-covered chair in the guest room.

"He went to visit his friends down the road, sir." Olúróunbí sent her knees to the ground again, a respectable distance from her father-in-law. "I will go and call him, right away, sir." She disappeared before he had a chance to respond and, in a flash, she was back with two ornamented burnt clay goblets filled with cool water. On both knees again, she offered each parent-in-law a goblet.

Màmá Ayọ̀ took the goblet from Olúróunbí bestowing upon her troubled countenance a smile that instantly rinsed off the visible apprehension from her face. Olúróunbí returned the smile and exhaled a sigh of gratitude. Olúróunbí always loved to see her mother-in-law. She remained her greatest ally within Ayọ̀'s large family. She always protected her from Bàbá Ayọ̀'s unyielding wrath, which erupted nine months after her matrimonial entry into Ayọ̀'s family. He had started nagging his wife before then when he did not observe what he had expected to see, a protruding belly. "Is your son's wife not carrying my grandson yet?" he would question Màmá Ayọ̀ from time to time. The response he got in her usual cheerful sultry voice infuriated him more.

"One would think you are announcing the opening of the annual festival the way you talk about your daughter-in-law's failure to give us grandchildren." He scowled, during one of such discussions. Màmá Ayọ̀ did not respond. She just plastered a smile on her face as if she had not heard his complaint. He threw his hands up in the air and just slumped into his seat and commenced to hum a song.

The dry-season dirt disturbed by the flip-flopping of Olúróunbí's goat-leather slippers toward Rótìmí's house had begun to cake her feet into ashy brownness. Rótìmí is Ayọ's closest friend in the town, and one of the few people who did not engage in gossip about Ayọ and Olúróunbí. He defended them vehemently—at times to the point of fighting. "Only useless and idle people spend their time gossiping and speculating about the lives of others," he had exploded once among fellow farmers while trekking home together from the farmlands. On some evenings, Ayọ joined Rótìmí and other men in the strategic and mathematical *ayò board* game under a thatched-roof shed for their evening after work to unwind and relax. This two-player board game had six holes on each side. The players had four pieces of dried non-edible seeds from the non-edible fruit *Sao* tree on each hole of the board to play with. Rótìmí, being the first player picked up the set of four pieces from his third hole on his side and dropped a seed on each hole during his turn ending on Ayọ's side. There was a pause. Ayọ calculated and decided to start his round from his second hole going clockwise, his piece landed on Rótìmí's second hole missing the losing empty hole. Each player took turns adding, subtracting and strategizing on the best moves to gain the most pieces in order to win the game.

Olúróunbí sighted her husband sitting on a wooden bench across from his friend with bent heads, the carved wooden board game *ọpọ́n ayò* sat between them. Under the thatched-roofed canopy shed, about six other men sat on a long bench beside Ayọ̀ and his friend, Rótìmí. The players were trying hard to focus on strategies to outwit each other, despite the distracting boisterous spectators. During this game event, the six supporters, siding with their favorite players, were unusually divided equally. Ayọ̀'s supporters teased Rótìmí ruthlessly, calling him *òpè* (the loser) while they crowned Ayọ̀ as *ọta* (the winner). During this fans' feud, Rótìmí's supporters did not relent in their effort to counter the opposing fans with witty and jovial comments. The evening pastime is a very important aspect of life in the land, Ayọ̀ enjoyed joining his friends and neighbors at the *ayò* spot from time to time. Olúróunbí heard the loud laughter of the men and the jovial teasing of the players, several houses away before she sighted the shed. Olúróunbí did not pay attention to the display of painted calabash gourds and drinking bowls nor the seller of the freshly blended assortment of fruits as she served customers.

As Ayọ̀ was about to pick up the victorious nine *ọmọ-ayò* game pieces that would have enabled the clearing of Rótìmí's pieces from his holes and knocked him out of the game, Olúróunbí's sudden cry-out from afar distracted him. Alarmed, he dropped the game pieces, sprang from the bench and sprinted towards her.

"What's wrong?" His brows furrowed, and his outstretched hands took her arms. "Are you all right?"

"*Màmá* and *Bàbá* have arrived," she announced as if forecasting a disaster.

"Which ones?" Ayọ̀ asked, first exhaling with relief that it was not worse, and then pretending not to have guessed which parents Olúróunbí's meant, judging from the worried look on her face.

He took her hand and walked her back to their compound. He squeezed and caressed her hand gently all the way. Upon entering the visitors' area and presenting himself before his parents, Ayọ̀ released Olúróunbí's hand and lowered his lanky body toward the floor in prostration.

His parents returned the greeting by placing their right hands on his head. "*Kú ìrọ̀lẹ́, ṣé daáda ni*? Good evening, how's everything? How was the farm today? I hope the sales yielded fruitful returns."

"Yes, sir. We thank Almighty God. Everything is good, sir."

After Ayọ̀ had assured his parents that all was well, he sauntered playfully toward his mother, bared his teeth, and winked at her. "I hope this old man is taking good care of you, *ooo*." He signaled at his father with a side nod.

"Who are you calling an old man, little boy?" retorted Bàbá Ayọ̀.

"Don't ever call my husband an old man. Okay, Ayọ̀? Your father is still young and strong. And yes, he's taking good care of me." She beamed and the men chuckled.

Ayọ̀ looked around and noticed that Olúróunbí had disappeared. He guessed she must have gone into the kitchen.

Bàbá Ayọ̀ cleared his throat. "Call your wife to come here. Tell her not to prepare any food for us tonight. We're not here for felicitation, okay?"

Ayọ̀ examined his parents' countenances and asked, "What's going on?"

Silence.

"Is everything all right?" He tried again. "Is everything okay, Bàbá mi?" He kept his eyes on his mother, trying to read her face but was not successful.

"Just summon your wife and stop querying me," Bàbá Ayọ̀ snapped and waved his son away.

Ayọ̀ obeyed and returned quickly with his wife, who looked like a goat being led to slaughter, even with Ayọ̀'s assurances that all would be well. Olúróunbí, head lowered with her chin resting on the top of her chest, took to her knees once again. Màmá Ayọ̀ faked a cough to get her husband's attention, and when he glanced at her, he got the message. As usual, she was silently imploring him to be gentle with their daughter-in-law. Slowly and deliberately, he directed his gaze to Olúróunbí and Ayọ̀, alternating between them.

"I am sure you are aware that we've been patiently waiting for you to produce our grandsons," he started then paused. He turned toward Olúróunbí and pinned his eyes on her face. "Till now, you have failed to make my son a man."

A strangulated squeak escaped from Olúróunbí. Ayọ̀, shaking his head, glared at his father in disbelief. "Ha-ha. Haba! Bàbá mi, how could you say such a thing, sir?"

"Bàbá Ayọ̀, please, please. Let's not blame anyone," interjected Màmá Ayọ̀. "That's not why we're here. We came to help them find a solution to the problem at hand. We all know that children come from God, not from the woman or the man."

"Well," Bàbá Ayọ̀ countered. "We don't know if there's a curse in her family preventing procreation. She might be one of the *ẹlẹ́gbẹ́* or *emèrè* (imps) who has been promised or betrothed to *okò ọrun* a celestial husband. I can't let her ruin my family. You know what's at stake, don't you?"

"Bàbá mi, I am not *emèrè ooo,* and I don't have any other husband in this world or above the sky except Ayò." Olúróunbí did not hide feeling offended.

"If you are not *emèrè* or *ẹlẹ́gbẹ́ ọrun* (imps), why haven't you conceived all these years that you have been wedded to my son, *hennn*?"

Ayò gave his father a scolding look, rose from his seat, and encircled one arm around Olúróunbí's shoulders. Noticing the wetness of her eyes, he said, "I'm so sorry. Please disregard what Papa just said," his voice quivered into her ear. He wrapped his other arm around her waist and started to help her from the kneeling position when sounds of footsteps were heard marching through the narrow corridor. They turned toward the entrance to the visitors' lounge, and their jaws dropped.

"*Ehen! Ẹrì pé alábòsí ni yín.* You are such a deceitful people." Màmá Olúróunbí stormed into the room followed by her husband, trudging behind her, his hands on her shoulders trying to prevent the entrance. With a strong shove from his wife, Bàbá Olúróunbí's hands fell off her shoulders to his sides. He attempted pulling her back with the tug of her *ìró (wrapper)*, but it was as futile as an ant trying to restrain the movement of an elephant.

"You invited us to a meeting here when the sun is at its zenith, and you're already here when the shadows are still in the front," Màmá Olúróunbí shouted at Ayọ̀'s parents. She was so infuriated she did not respond to Olúróunbí's and Ayọ̀'s greetings.

"*Ẹmá bìnú ooo*, my in-laws. We're sorry. We were coming from somewhere, and it just happened that we got done earlier, so we headed here." Màmá Ayọ̀ responded apologetically while Bàbá Ayọ̀ continually shook his head, trying to stem his temper.

"*Ẹjọ̀* please, I don't want to hear any story. You planned to get here sooner so you could rain abuses on our daughter."

"Mama mi." Olúróunbí darted in front of her mother and hugged her tighter than normal. "*Ẹkáàsán*, good afternoon, *mà*." She held her mother in place with her body. "Mama mi, please, don't!" she whispered. Ayọ̀ stood close to his wife, flanking his mother-in-law on the right while his father-in-law's position encapsulated Màmá Olúróunbí, preventing further aggression toward Ayọ̀'s parents.

As if seeing her daughter for the first time since she entered her home, she pulled her head back and gazed into her eyes, the tension in her body dissipating as fast as it had come. The sayings of the elderly wise that "if the ears did not hear anything bad, sadness would not overcome the inside" came to mind as Màmá Olúróunbí recalled hearing Bàbá Ayọ̀ berating her daughter. *How could he have concluded that it's my daughter who is unable to conceive? It could be his son with the problem.* Màmá Olúróunbí mean-mugged and rolled her eyes multiple times at Bàbá Ayọ̀ and produced a loud hissing for all to hear.

Bàbá Ayọ̀ stood up and returned the mean-mugging. "Listen, I don't have the patience for all this foolishness, okay. The reason why I called this meeting is to give your daughter, Olúróunbí, the last chance to prove herself a woman."

"*What?* Are you mad, Bàbá Ayọ̀?"

"I must have been to have allowed my son to marry your daughter," he spat. "But now, I'm back to my senses."

Bàbá Olúróunbí released his wife and walked up to Bàbá Ayọ̀, standing a few inches away at eye level. "Listen *Ọ̀gbẹ́ni*, in your life—I repeat—in your life, and as long as you live, don't you ever talk to my wife and daughter like that again, okay?" Bàbá Ayọ̀ took a step back and stared speechlessly at his counterpart. He had never seen him like this before nor imagined that he could stand up to anybody. "Do I make myself clear to you?" The uncharacteristic fierce and authoritative depth of his voice filled the silence of the room. Bàbá Ayọ̀ could not find his voice.

He was not the only one in a stupor; everyone in the room stared at Bàbá Olúróunbí, whose shoulders seemed to have added layers of muscles.

Màmá Ayọ̀ was the first to regain her composure. *"Eh-hen-hum, Ẹmá bìnú, ànọ mi daada.* My honorable in-law, please. Don't be annoyed. Our relationship will never be destroyed. We're sorry. Everyone, please, let's not argue. Let's sit down and help our children find a good solution to their situation." She pulled her husband onto his seat and took hers beside him.

Màmá Olúróunbí's taut, ready-to-fight muscles melted like shea butter in the hot tropical sun. She stared at her husband, strutting across the room towards his seat. Pleasantly shocked, her dropped jaw curved up into a rare beam as she continued to gaze at her husband of thirty-four years. She had never seen him display such valor before. She allowed Olúróunbí and Ayọ̀ to lead her to a seat facing the Àjàní family.

As if agreed and rehearsed, the young couple exchanged a smile, a nod, and a sigh of relief in synchronized choreography.

"Hmm...hmm," Ayọ̀ interrupted the awkward silence with the clearing of his throat. "Our dear parents, it makes us sad to see you bickering over the situation. We have become one family, and we need to be a united family, continuing to pray. Olúróunbí and I are confident that the time for our precious children to be born has just not arrived yet. Simple as that." Ayọ̀ looked over at his wife as he spoke. He was encouraged by the multiple nods of her head in agreement and gratitude. He continued. "We're looking up to you, our dear parents, to counsel us and give us hope."

"We've been doing that for over three years, but your wife refused to bear any child. How long do we have to pray and wait for her?" his father interrupted. Two parallel veins on his temple seemed like they were about to burst open under his skin. His eyes blazed with fury on his contorted face.

Olúróunbí feared her father-in-law was warming up for another round of an altercation.

The more Ayọ̀ pleaded for an amicable dialogue, the more it seemed to infuriate his father.

Nonetheless, he intensified his pleas and signaled to his mother for assistance in calming his father down, a signal she did not miss.

Màmá Ayọ̀, cognizant of the effect of her persuasive skills on her husband, was also aware of her contextual limitations. Some of her interventions had produced the desired result, but others had the opposite effect Therefore, she had to be careful when intervening so that he would not perceive her as an antagonist. Tentatively, Màmá Ayọ̀'s hand crept from her thigh onto Bàbá Ayọ̀'s thigh, found and took one of his hands, and gave it a firm squeeze. He ignored it and continued his tirade. She squeezed it a bit tighter. And he ignored her again as if he had not felt it.

He whipped his head toward her, raising his voice as if making an announcement in the Ìlúgidi town square. "Màmá Ayọ̀! I need to tell your son the seriousness of the situation." He continued to fume. "If it takes a potential madman ten years to prepare for insanity, how many years would he then get to spend in the actual insanity itself? Ha-ha. How long will Olúróunbí spend in my son's home, preparing for pregnancy? If Olúróunbí is not capable of producing my grandson, Ayọ̀ must send her back to her father's house, so he can marry another woman who has many sons in her womb waiting to be born."

"Ha!"

"Ha! *Kínì*? Why is your mouth hanging ajar?"

"Don't you know that we are your in-laws? *Orò Jàno, ooo*; an in-law is a figure to be feared, cherished and respected ... I have warned you not to disrespect my family again, you! insolent man! You have no decorum and no respect for anyone, yourself included. Otherwise, you wouldn't be talking like this."

Màmá Olúróunbí led the way to her daughter's and son-in-law's large bedroom. "Olúróunbí, come over here right now, go inside the room, and pack all your belongings. You are leaving this house today. You are no longer the wife of this foolish man's son, henceforth."

At that moment, everybody started talking and shouting at the same time, and nobody could understand the insults and counter-insults directed at one another. Then, the voices ceased at once to hear what the others were saying but started up again simultaneously.

Suddenly, a deep male voice seemed to emit from the walls of the room stating, *"ÓTÓ! ENOUGH!"* In auto-obedience, everyone stopped talking as sudden as they had started earlier. They looked around in confusion, trying to determine where the voice had come from. Then they saw that the command had come from Ayọ̀, who had spoken into the pillar that stood in the center of the room. The architectural construction of the brick stone pillar with small carved out holes rose to the apex of the high ceiling of the house. It was through these holes that Ayọ̀'s amplified voice traveled to the ceiling, dispersed down into the walls, and then divulged into the room with surrounding effect. The shock that registered on their faces pleased Ayọ̀. He continued with his directives immediately. "I'm asking our parents to excuse themselves from our home at this moment. This visit is over!"

Olúróunbí strode over to her husband and stood next to him, showing where her alliance belonged. Ayọ̀ extended his arm and draped it around her shoulders.

The first person to respond was Màmá Olúróunbí. "If you know what's good for you, you will obey me and pack your things right now and follow us back home. This is not a family to be with for the rest of your life."

"This is my home for life, Mama mi. I'm sorry, but I'm not leaving my husband."

"Yes, you are. If I'm the one who carried you for nine months in my womb and wrapped you on my back for more than two years, you will obey me and get out of this house right now."

"My daughter is not packing out of her husband's house, Màmá Olúróunbí. Don't make such an abominable statement," Bàbá Olúróunbí declared.

Màmá Olúróunbí glared at her husband. "Are you implying that Olúróunbí should stay after all the abomination that this uncultured man has said to our daughter and in our presence?"

"I am not implying it, I am declaring it. Olúróunbí will not abandon her marriage because of her father-in-law's thoughtless words and careless behavior."

"Thank you very much, Bàbá Olúróunbí for exhibiting maturity," injected Mama Ayo. "My daughter-in-law is not going anywhere. This is her home!" She stomped one of her feet on the floor.

"No, it's no longer her home," Bubbles of saliva emanated from Baba Ayo's mouth as he yelled. "She's following her parents out of this house, today because they deceived us. They hid the truth that their daughter is barren from us."

Màmá Ayọ̀ shot her husband a look that she thought would silence him as it would any sensible man, but instead, it removed all the sensibility in him at that moment. "You must stop being so insulting to our in-laws. What's wrong with you today, he-e-en?"

Baba Ayo glared at his wife. "Nothing is wrong with me. It's you who's not with your senses, he retorted before turning back to the Odetayos. "I'm declaring this marriage dissolved from this moment on!" He turned to face Ayọ̀ who was shaking his head while holding on tightly to Olúróunbí. Ayọ̀ deliberately stepped back, wondering if his father would go as far as yanking her from him. When Bàbá Ayọ̀ glanced at Olúróunbí's damp face and quivering lips, he quickly looked away. "If you know what's good for you, Ayọ̀ *ọmọ* Àjàní! You'd release her to gather her belongings and follow her parents."

"Father!" shouted Ayọ̀. "Sir, that's enough. With all due respect, you need to take your leave now, as I said earlier, sir. What you're doing is unacceptable. How can you speak to the parents of my WIFE in such manner, sir? It's unfair, sir." Bàbá Ayọ̀ noticed that his son's face had contorted with anger and grief at the same time, but he looked away.

"This man has been afflicted with serious madness!" Màmá Olúróunbí, eyes blazing with rage, yelled.

"Màmá mi, please. Don't insult my father-in-law, ma, … please, ma," Olúróunbí countered. "He's *Bàbá ọkọ mi. As you and Bàbá mi raised me,*

Bàbá ọkọ eni; Bàbá eni ni. My husband's father is my father." Hands clasped, eyes imploring, knees bent, Olúróunbí beseeched her mother. "Please, ma."

"Who? This one?" Màmá Olúróunbí pointed a disdainful left finger at Bàbá Ayọ. "This man is not worthy to be your father-in-law. He's no longer your father-in-law from this moment on," she shrieked without taking her glare of off Bàbá Ayọ's face.

Bàbá Olúróunbí grabbed his wife's arm and covered her mouth with the other hand. "Stop! Stop making such pronouncements."

Màmá Ayọ also grabbed her husband's *agbádá (Men's flowy garment over top and bottom)* roughly and pulled him away. "Don't make such a pronouncement. You know that evil spirits may hear you and wish it to be so. Don't allow *Ìbìlísù* to whisper things that could destroy the family into your mind *ooo. Haba!* Bàbá Ayọ!" Her face was contorted into a mix of anger and disbelief.

"Yes, sir. Mama mi is right, sir. Please, watch your words, sir. This is so unfair, sir."

"That's right! I'm watching my words and that's what would happen. I need you to give me a grandson, and I'm not waiting any longer for someone who is incapable of bearing children."

"You know what? It's not my daughter who cannot bear children; it's your son who cannot impregnate a woman."

Bàbá Ayọ̀'s chest started heaving up and down, head shaking rapidly from side to side, while his protruding deep brown pupils seemed to darken a shade, almost popping out of their sockets. He brought up an opened palm, lurched forward at Màmá Olúróunbí, aiming for a 'dirty slap,' but Bàbá Olúróunbí was faster. He extended his strong right hand and blocked the attempt. He then moved in with his body for a collision. The impact made him think that he had run into a tree trunk. Màmá Ayọ̀ had also pulled at her husband's *agbádá* to prevent the movement. At that point, Ayọ̀ stepped in, picked up his father as if he was a little lad, and briskly carried him toward the corridor with his mother at his heels. He did not stop until they were outside the compound. It happened so fast that Bàbá Ayọ̀ did not get a chance to utter a word nor wiggle any part of his body in protest. Ayọ̀ allowed his feet to touch the ground, wrapped his right arm around his *bùbá* and *agbádá* covered frame, and tucked the other hand under his arm, leading him in a forward march toward his parents' home. Panting, Màmá Ayọ̀ scurried along in silence. Without pausing, they grunted their replies to people who greeted them as they passed by along the road, causing questioning stares behind them.

The Àjàní s lived in the central part of Ìlúgidi, near many of the small convenient markets, the palace of Ọba Ìlúgidi, the festival town square, and other important community structures, except the town's central market, Alátùnṣe, which was strategically situated at the entrance of the town. That way, it made it easier for neighboring town folks and villagers to navigate. It was also meant to prevent unwanted elements from the possible assault on its people.

Upon arrival at the family quad-shaped compound, Ayọ̀ reduced the pace at which they had pranced down the road, hurriedly returning the *Ẹ̀káàbọ̀* greetings just as his mother did. Bàbá Ayọ̀, on the other hand, did not utter a sound. They entered the biggest house in the compound and Ayọ̀ offered his *Ìdọ̀bálẹ̀* adieu greetings and exited immediately, not minding his father's ignorance of his prostration. He hurried back onto the road like a warrior on an urgent mission to defend his land.

Soon enough, Ayọ̀ entered his house and found his in-laws sitting and talking to one another. He offered his *Ìdọ̀bálẹ̀* greetings and then started to speak. "Please, *Bàbá wa and Màmá wa*, I'd like you to take your leave now, please sir, please Ma." His voice came off deeper and assertive.

As Màmá Olúróunbí started to utter what sounded like a protest, Olúróunbí grabbed her mother by the hand, nodded at her father, and together they escorted Màmá Olúróunbí through the corridor into the front yard and onto the pedway that led to the other side of town. Bàbá Olúróunbí took his wife's hand from his daughter and sent her back to her house. "My daughter! go back to your husband and apologize to him for your

Màmá's unexcused behavior today. Please, tell him that I'm very sorry and that such a thing will never happen again. I promise."

"*Ẹ seun,* sir. Thank you very much, sir." She flashed her father a smile of gratitude. She looked at her mother with pleading eyes. "Please, don't be cross, Mama mi, everything will be alright. Just have faith, please."

Màmá Olúróunbí rolled her eyes, hissed, shrugged, and followed her husband's lead like an obedient old dog.

Olúróunbí ran inside her house, covering the corridor in a flash and found her husband leaning against the pillar in the middle of the room.

Olúróunbí approached her husband and held him by the waist as she went on her knees.

"I'm very sorry about how my mother acted today. Please excuse her behavior for my sake."

Ayọ̀ reached out and pulled his wife off her feet. "I am the one who's supposed to be sorry for what my father did. Please forgive all that he said about you. I really hate it when he gets that way. My mother is the levelheaded one and she always tries to get him to behave better. But sometimes he's so out of control that even my mother can't stop his rampage." He placed his hand at the back of her head and laid it on his shoulder while stroking his apologies into her back.

Olúróunbí draped her arms around her husband's neck and pressed her body into his. "Same thing with my mother; my father is also the levelheaded one and he tries to get her to behave better. She believes that my father is too gentle, and that people take advantage of him as a result. Therefore, she is always ready to fight a battle for him even if there are no issues or battles to fight."

"What a day this has been." Ayọ̀ sighed. "Let's go and rest our bodies for a while this afternoon."

"I agree. My knees are hurting from kneeling down and begging our parents not to quarrel. You know something, my darling Olówó orí mi, the owner of my crown?"

"Tell me."

"Have you observed that my mom and your dad are very similar? Aren't they so much alike?"

Ayọ̀ exploded in boisterous laughter. "Of course, I have observed that. Imagine if they had been husband and wife."

"Ha! It would have been fire and fire all the time. Their home would be nicknamed 'House of Fire' with daily fire bolts hurling." Olúróunbí joined her husband in the laughter. "However, the elders say that *'tí irin ba kan irin, ìkan á tẹ̀ fún ìkan ni.'* I've literally seen it at Bàbá Alagbede the blacksmith's workshop. My father had sent me to collect an iron tool from him. When I got there, he was pressing the tips of two thick iron pieces against each other in an open flame. After some time, one of the irons gave way and bent downwards."

"Yes, that's how it is," he responded.

Side by side, arms around each other, they walked slowly into their bedroom and sat on the bed for a moment before easing their weary bodies into a sleeping position.

The following morning, Bàbá Ayọ̀ summoned his wife to his presence after she had served his breakfast of *ògì Àkàmù* and *mọ́ín-mọ́ín.* They had gone to bed without talking after the forceful return from their son's home. Both husband and wife had very restless sleep in their respective rooms. They had offered their pre-sunrise prayers separately instead of the usual practice as one unit. Màmá Ayọ̀ asked her husband to eat before talking about anything, but he insisted that it was impossible for him to eat without divulging what lay in his chest.

"*Aya mi olóríire.* Firstly, I am so ashamed of my behavior yesterday toward our daughter-in-law and *àwọn ànọ wa* who are honorable in-laws. I regret it, especially how I failed to regard my son's feelings. I hope he will find it in his heart to forgive me." He raised his head and looked at Màmá Ayọ̀.

What she saw drawn on his face hit her heart harder than what she felt witnessing her husband's despicable display at their son's home. It was a combination of distress, worry, and regret. Màmá Ayọ̀ then knew that there was more to this than Olúróunbí and Ayọ̀'s childlessness. Instantly, she brushed her feelings aside and pulled her short four-legged sturdy wooden *àpótí* closer to her husband, giving him her full attention. "I'm all ears, my husband."

Bàbá Ayọ̀ inhaled heavily and started. "What I'm about to tell you is top secret that only a handful of elders in the seven unified towns know about. And this might explain the reason for my irrational behavior yesterday."

"Uhmm. I'm listening. Go on, *ọkọ mi.* (my husband)"

He looked around as if checking to see if somebody was nearby. He appeared uneasy and stood up abruptly, picking up a casual *aṣọ-òkè* hat and taking Màmá Ayọ̀'s hand. They started toward the door. "The walls have ears," he pronounced as they exited the day room into the courtyard and toward the gateless compound entrance. They walked in silence for a few minutes until they got to an intersection with no houses nor bushes close by. Bàbá Ayọ̀ stopped and made a 360-degree check. Satisfied that no one was within hearing, he started to talk fast.

"As you know, we have an ancient kingdom comprising of two large towns and five villages of varying sizes and populations."

"Yes, yes, yes." She nodded impatiently.

"These twin towns rule the union based on a certain complicated tradition that had been laid down since time immemorial. You know the two towns referenced, right?"

"Of course, I do. The town of Kẹ́lẹ́gbẹ́ and our town, Ìlúgidi."

"Do you know how the ruling town and the ruling family is selected?" Bàbá Ayọ̀ challenged his wife.

"I heard it's rotated by turns between the two towns, but I don't know how the ruling family is determined."

"All right. That's what I will explain to you today and how it concerns us."

Màmá Ayọ̀ tilted her head bringing her right ear closer to her husband's mouth.

"Yes, you're right. The throne is rotated between the two towns quite all right. However, the ruling dynasty is determined by the birth of the first grandson from the first son of the Grand-Balógun commander. It is that grandson who will be raised and trained from infancy as the custodian and king of the united seven communities. However, if the Grand-Balógun commander's first son fails to produce a son as his firstborn, the town will have missed the opportunity to the throne. The opposing town would then be given the advantage of two consecutive reigns. It has happened many times over centuries."

"Ha!" Màmá Ayọ̀ started nodding repeatedly.

Bàbá Ayọ̀ watched as her face lit up, then furrowed and later appeared confused. "But we are the current—"

"Yes, I know what you're thinking. Our great town Ìlúgidi is ruling now. The problem is that the reign has skipped Ìlúgidi too many times. The elders have met and decided that Ìlúgidi must not lose the throne again and that the monarch must remain here for as long as possible. The next eligible heir to the throne is selected to be the first son of Ayọ̀. He doesn't know that because no one is supposed to know, except the current Ọba and a group of four elders and myself in this town; as well as four selective elders and the head of Àjàkayé 's household, which is Bàbá Bámijí'. So, since I'm not telling Ayọ̀, I'm not breaking the rules. Besides, I'm only telling you so that you can understand the reason behind my behavior and, I need you to support me to make sure Ayọ̀ gives birth to a son as quickly as possible. Olúróunbí might not have the destiny to become a mother. The sovereignty of our town lies in our hands. We can't afford to lose the opportunity."

Màmá Ayọ̀'s eyes had widened to its full capacity as she listened to her husband's narrative. She attempted to speak but only incomprehensible blabbers came out of her mouth.

They heard footsteps coming towards them. Bàbá Ayọ̀ tapped at his mouth in a gesture to be quiet, took her hands and led her back to the compound and into their house in silence.

Chapter Four
ÌDÙNNÚ ÀTI ẸKÚN - JOY AND TEARS

Màmá Olúróunbí ran around her daughter's room screaming like a mouse pursued by a hungry cat. Ayọ̀ tried to catch her and hold her in place.

"Màmá, wait! Please, stop running around the room. Neighbors will hear your voice and they'll think you are being hurt."

Olúróunbí could not control the laughter that was making her bulging stomach bounce and shake up and down. Watching her mother run and jump up and down hysterically made her eyes flush out streams of tears.

Finally, Ayọ̀ caught up with his mother-in-law and sat her down at the edge of their bed right beside her daughter.

Màmá Olúróunbí's arms flew out and wrapped her daughter in her arms sobbing, singing, dancing, and kissing her simultaneously. *"Ọlọ́run ọṣé ooo. Olúwa ọṣé ooo. Modúpẹ́ ooo."* She repeatedly thanked God as more tears streamed out of her eyes down her face onto the *bùbá top of the àdìrẹ* (tie and dye outfit). "God has slapped the mouths of my enemies shut. Thank you for shutting up the mouths of the gossipers and those who condemned my daughter to the life of a barren woman. Àwọn *aroni pin (Haters)*."

Olúróunbí could not tell if her mother was laughing or crying or doing both simultaneously.

"Stop crying; it's God's Will that I will become a mother." She smiled through her tears.

"I am grateful to God that all the people who said I was not a real man have also been silenced. Both my wife and I have been vindicated from people's accusations. Some people can be so cruel and unempathetic. They threw so many hurtful things at us as if we were responsible for procreation. They should know that God is the only one who determines people's destiny."

"You are right, my son. I am sorry I was one of those people. It was your father who made me spit out such a statement during our last meeting and argument. I always knew that you are a real man."

"You did?" Ayọ̀ queried hopefully.

"Yes, my son. I knew you were a real man all along."

"How did you know, Ma?" Ayọ̀ raised an eyebrow. Then he glanced back and forth from mother to daughter. He rested his gaze on Olúróunbí who averted her smiling face.

"Your wife told me from the day you made her a woman."

The threesome broke out in laughter at the same time.

"So, how far are you, my daughter?

"It's been six new moons, Ma."

"How could you have stayed away from me for that long?"

"We're sorry, Ma," Ayọ̀ interjected. "We decided to keep her within the compound away from everybody until we were sure. I just don't want her to be stressed at all. My parents haven't seen her yet. They also don't know."

Olúróunbí added, *"Ẹmá bìnú,* we apologize, Mama mi. The only person who knows is Ìyá Àbíye, the midwife. She comes here regularly and takes care of me and the baby."

"*Mi ò bínú.* I'm not upset, I understand. Besides, I'm too happy to be upset." Hands outstretched, she raised her face upwards and mouthed some prayers. She returned her gaze to Olúróunbí and stated, "Please, take it easy. I will be coming to help you cook every day henceforth."

Olúróunbí and Ayọ̀ nodded their acquiescence.

"When are you going to inform my in-laws?" Màmá Olúróunbí smiled at Ayọ̀.

"Tomorrow, Ma. I will go and apologize to them and bring them over. I am sure they will forgive my rudeness in the way I escorted them home once they find out that we are having a baby soon."

"Yes. I am sure they will discard their anger immediately." Màmá Olúróunbí picked up her handbag. "Let me get back home quickly and give my husband this wonderful news. I will be back tomorrow to make you *ògì ati mọ́ín-mọ́ín, Olúróunbí ọmọ mi olóríire (My blessed child).*"

Olúróunbí and Ayọ̀ walked her to the door from which Màmá Olúróunbí sent her daughter back inside. Ayọ̀ escorted his mother-in-law for a few minutes before Màmá Olúróunbí excused him and sent him back home.

Chapter Five
ÌWÁYÉ OLÚFÚNMI – ARRIVAL OF OLÚFÚNMI

One Friday morning in Ìlúgidi, the sky was full of clouds, yet the sun forced its way through, giving the town a rayless brightness. The rainfall was light, but enough to dampen the clothes of the people walking in it and caused the furry animals to occasionally shake the wetness off their bodies. The birds and other animals seemed more quiet than usual. Even the roosters seemed lazy and reluctant to compete in their usual crows at dawn. The atmosphere was tranquil.

Olúróunbí and Ayọ̀ had risen from sleep, washed up, and commenced their morning routine supplication. Ayọ̀ was not surprised that Olúróunbí could not place her forehead onto the ground in their usual ritual worship. She had stopped trying to prostrate on the floor about two or three months ago because her belly had protruded so much that it became impossible. So, she sat on a stool while Ayọ̀ did the prostration. On this morning, however, his ears seemed to be picking out some grunting and ruffling of cloth, affecting his concentration. His eyes kept darting sideways at his wife. He sensed that she was uncomfortable but could not break the prayers. As soon as they rounded up the dawn prayer, Ayọ̀ hurried to Olúróunbí's side. He saw that she was in serious discomfort. Her nostrils flared, and her eyes were squeezed shut to push out the pain. She let out grunts several times louder than when they were praying. "My sweet, what's wrong?" he asked in a tremulous voice. "Are you okay?"

Olúróunbí responded with a series of louder and deeper grunts. The alien sound sent strange waves into Ayọ̀'s head, running through his body to his toes.

He jumped to his feet, placed his hands under his wife's arms and carefully assisted her to her feet. "*Pẹ̀lẹ́...pẹ̀lẹ́...pẹ̀lẹ́,*" he offered repeatedly as he led her slowly to their bed. "I think it's time. Let me go and fetch Ìyá Àbíye *kíá kíá (hurriedly)—.*"

Olúróunbí responded with louder grunts, nods, and a wave of her hand.

"Will you be okay, my love?"

The stern glare from her suddenly enlarged almond eyes sent him scurrying toward the door. He quickly made an about-turn and rushed back to the bedside, placing his hands on her shoulder and belly, trying to comfort her. He was reluctant to leave her alone. The scream, "Go now and bring Ìyá Àbíye right now!" sent him instantly back to the door.

"Hey! *Mo dáràn (I am in trouble)!*" He squirmed at her uncharacteristic command before fleeing the room. At the corridor, he perambulated between the entrance and the visitor's room until he heard Olúróunbí shouting again from the room to hurry up in bringing the midwife. "Okay...okay. I'm going now. I just don't want to leave you in the house all alone, dear."

"Go! Hurry! Please," she pleaded this time.

Ayọ̀ rushed out of the house and took to his heels as he did when he was a little boy. He was not aware of, nor did he care about, the inquisitive stares from neighbors who were engaged in yard sweeping or using their chewing sticks outside their houses. As he turned the corner toward Ìyá Àbíye's house at the end of the road, he bumped into one of his fellow farmers, Akin-lọmọ, knocking him, his basket, and his tools to the ground. "I'm sorry *oooo*," he said without pausing in his stride. "Akin-lọmọ, please go to Màmá Olúróunbí's house and tell her to come to our house immediately. Her daughter needs her right away." Ayọ̀ did not stop walking briskly as he sent Akin-lọmọ on the errand. "After that, run to my parent's house and tell them to meet me at my house. I'm going to Ìyá Àbíye's house. Thank you, *ore mi*, Akin." He increased his run-walking pace.

Akin-lọmọ picked himself off the ground, gathered his scattered tools and basket, and shouted gleefully back at Ayọ̀. "I am there already. Our wife will deliver safely *ooo*." He sprinted toward Màmá Olúróunbí's house instantly.

At Ìyá Àbíye's house, Ayọ̀ provided the midwife with a status update on Olúróunbí's condition after which he left and headed back to his house.

"Please, hurry up, Ma. I need to be with my wife until you get there. She's home alone right now.

Ẹjọ̀wọ́ mà, ẹmá pẹ̀, mà ooo (Please come back quickly)."

"Don't worry; I will be there soon. You just go. I will gather my things and meet up with you soon," replied the midwife as she entered an inner room and started collecting the necessary items into a cow-leather pouch.

By the time Ayọ̀ returned to his house, Olúróunbí's condition had worsened. He saw that she was covered in sweat, her face was riddled with suffering, and her body with tremors. At first, he did not notice their neighbor, Màmá Bídèmí, fanning Olúróunbí with a feather *abẹ̀bẹ̀* fan with one hand and holding her hand with the other.

"*Pẹ̀lẹ́...pẹ̀lẹ́...pẹ̀lẹ́, rọ́ọ́jú.* Sorry, please, persevere patiently. Don't cry. Continue to persevere. Just don't cry. It's forbidden for a woman in labor to cry. Just focus on your unborn baby and pray. Just continue to pray."

Ayọ̀ stared at Màmá Bídèmí as if she was speaking a language other than *Yorùbá.* Confusion had gripped his senses. He turned around suddenly at the sound of a person's entrance. He felt a sense of relief at the sight of his mother-in-law who rushed straight to the bedside. Next came in Màmá Abiye, the midwife.

The first thing she did was send Ayọ̀ out of the bedroom and instructed him to wait outside the house until he was summoned. He was told to engage in prayers for the safe delivery of his child and the health of his wife.

As Ayọ̀ paced up and down the length of the front yard of his house, his parents arrived. His mother patted him on the shoulder and told him to recite prayers for the safe delivery of the baby before entering the house. Father and son stared at each other for some time in silence. They felt each other's tension and worries. Bàbá Ayọ̀ was worried for two reasons. He was worried about his son's worries, and he was worried about the gender of the expected baby. He had two prayers in his heart: the safe delivery of mother and baby and the arrival of his first grandson. His heart was pounding so loud he thought Ayọ̀ could hear it. He could not bear the thought of this child to be other than a male. It had to be a boy so that his life's mission would come true.

Ayọ̀ was unaware of the expectation that he was supposed to give birth to the next protector of the Ìlúgidi sovereignty. Ayọ̀ thought that whenever his father referred to his unborn child as a male, he thought his father was just partial to males as the firstborn like most typical Yorùbá men. He never argued with him, but Ayọ̀ had no preference for male or female. He only hoped that he would have sons and daughters. Ayọ̀ was not privy to the history of the two families that had been chosen a long time ago who had the right to the crown of the custodian and protector of the sovereignty of the seven circular towns and villages. The position was the most revered in this land mass, except that of the oba, or kings. It carried spiritual, financial, security responsibilities, and prestige. Bàbá Ayọ̀, being the head of the Àjàní Family, had been eagerly expecting his firstborn, Ayọ̀, to give birth to a son before the other candidate did since his nineteenth birthday.

Bàbá Ayọ̀ grabbed Ayọ̀ by the arm and pulled him into a firm embrace, an embrace that he needed as much as his son did.

Ayọ̀ succumbed to the fatherly embrace, releasing his tensed muscles into his father's softer, aged muscles. "Thank you, sir," he said as he reluctantly released himself from the folds of his father's *agbádá (Men's flowy garment)*. "Can I go inside and see how my wife is doing?" Ayọ̀ asked, sounding like a little boy who was asking if he could go outside and play.

"No…no, you can't. The women will chase you out even before you get to the door."

Ayọ̀ could not stay still. His knees seemed to be shaking involuntarily; his hands began to clasp and unclasp, rubbing against each other in a prayer-like, pleading gesture. His ears stood up, straining to hear the sounds through the wall outside his bedroom. He could hear sounds, voices, and movements, but could not make out what was being said. He sprang to his feet and headed determinedly toward the door. As soon as he placed one foot on the doorstep, he almost bumped into his mother who was rushing toward the door at the same time.

"*Akú ewu ọmọ oooo!*" she shouted. "Congratulations to us, we have given birth to a big baby. *Ọmọ olóríire,* our blessing has arrived, and it's fully formed and healthy!" She continued to shout at the top of her lungs. "*Akú oríire ooo. Gbogbo ará àdúgbò, ẹbá wa yọ̀ ooo! Ati bímọ ooo. (Friends and neighbors, come and rejoice with us on the arrival of our newborn baby,)*"

Ayọ̀, taking his mother's cue, started shouting and trying to get past her at the doorway. He picked her up and hugged her.

Bàbá Ayọ̀ had also sprung to his feet and had joined the duo at the doorway, his joyful shouts mixing into the commotion.

Ayọ̀ put his mother down and flew into his house, headed straight to the birthing room. He rushed inside and froze in stride at the spectacle that presented itself before him. He saw his wife, lying on her back, trying to steady her breathing. A bundle wrapped in white cotton cloth was placed on her chest while Ìyá Àbíye and Màmá Olúróunbí were busy cleaning and massaging her stomach. The bundle was screaming at the top of its tiny lungs while Olúróunbí cradled it to her bosom. Ayọ̀ knew this was the most beautiful sound that he had ever heard in his life.

Olúróunbí could never have imagined the look she saw drawn on her husband's face. Whatever joy he was feeling was perfectly displayed for anyone to see. His protruding round eyes became even larger. The happy beats of his heart had drowned out congratulatory greetings from the women in the room. He inched closer until he found himself looking at what he believed was the most beautiful face on earth. He was looking at his baby for the first time. Bending, he stared at the copper-colored face, tiny buttoned nose, and reddish parted lips from which a tiny pink tongue emitted the sweet yelling. The yelling gradually stopped when Ayọ̀ laid one hand on it while cuddling Olúróunbí with the other. He rocked them very gently. He was not aware that his eyes had squeezed out tears until a couple dropped onto Olúróunbí's chest. "Thank you, God!" he whispered. "Thank you, *ẹ seun, aya mi àtàtà*, my darling wife. Thank you for making me a father to this most beautiful human creation. Thank you, so, so much. Lord, I'm very grateful to you."

"*Akú oríire ńlá yí,*" Olúróunbí said in a tired voice, gazing into her husband's wet eyes. "The Creator did it. He gave us this beautiful gift."

Ayọ̀ nodded his agreement thoughtfully. *Indeed!* Olúwafúnwa. Tears moistened his eyes again, even though his countenance was a picture of immense happiness. He could not take his eyes off the little human being in his wife's arms, who looked like the inside of ripe pawpaw in an angelic human form. He had just found out that love at first sight indeed existed.

Olúróunbí realized that miraculously all the unbearable pain had disappeared. After her baby came out, the incredible pain came out with it. Ìyá Àbíye the midwife simply pressed down on her belly, and the placenta eased itself out. She felt instant relief and offloaded. She could not keep her eyes off the soft, delicate flesh placed on her bare skin.

Meanwhile, outside the house, the situation has taken a bizarre turn. Bàbá Ayọ̀ asked his wife again the sex of the new baby, and she replied as joyfully as expected. "It's a girl! A most beautiful girl! She looks like a doll made of gold and—"

Bàbá Ayọ̀ raised his palm at his wife's face, motioning her to silence. "What do you mean a girl?"

"I mean we have been blessed with a charming granddaughter." She knew what her husband was driving.

"A girl? The baby is a girl, not a boy! *Yeeeeeeh*!"

With those utterances, Bàbá Ayọ̀ jumped off the ground and then flopped himself onto the ground, landing on his rear end.

Chapter Six

BÀBÁ AYọ̀ TọRọ ÀFORÍJÌ - BÀBÁ AYọ̀ OFFERED PROPITIATION

Some of the elders who had witnessed Bàbá Ayọ̀'s reaction to the birth of the baby girl had taken the case to the palace and had reported it to the king. They requested for the (king) *oba's* intervention in resolving the family matter. Ọba Ìlúgidi had summoned Bàbá Ayọ̀ to hear his side of the story. Ọba Ìlúgidi was one of the few people who were privy to the secret of the custodian of the sovereignty. The Ọba told him that he shared and understood his sentiment but counseled him against the approach he was using. "Enmity with your family will not solve the problem. You must apply wisdom and gentle maneuvering for the desired result. Your method may alienate your son and all hope for our land will be lost."

Bàbá Ayọ̀ accepted the king's advice and went with his wife to offer his apology. Both Ayọ̀ and

Olúróunbí accepted the offering. Family reconciliation took place, and all was well.

By and by, the family had a naming ceremony, and it was attended by well-wishers, as well as inquisitive and nosy people of the town who wanted to see if it was really Olúróunbí and Ayọ̀ who had a child. Some doubted that the couple really had a baby of their own because they had not seen Olúróunbí during her pregnancy. Not until the pregnancy was very advanced did, she venture out of the compound. Some of the people who lived close by had seen her around the compound and the nearby mini market that she got the basics for daily cooking. She had noticed the shock on their faces, their hands covering their mouths with surprise. The news was spread throughout the town.

A lot of drummers and percussionists invited themselves to the naming ceremony, joining the celebrants' drummers. The selected elders, religious custodians, chiefs representing the Ọba, and a palace courtier officiated the ceremony. The baby was given several special names by key members of Olúróunbí and Ayọ̀'s families. Food and drinks were in abundance for all the guests. Pouches of cowry shells, silver, and gold coins were in high circulation per traditional appreciation and demonstration of the happy occasion.

To Olúróunbí's pleasant surprise, Bàbá Ayọ̀ even showered the musicians and the new parents with riches. He had proven that his propitiation was genuine.

The baby's primary name was Olúfúnmi, which means, "God giveth to me." Everyone noticed the unique redness of her skin. It was likened to the redness of palm oil; thus, she was soon nicknamed *Ọmọ-pupa-apọ́n-bí-epo* (child-as-red-as-palm-oil). The parents and grandparents settled into their new roles of caring for and raising Olúfúnmi. Everyone doted on her, even some of the people of Ìlúgidi who had stigmatized Olúróunbí as a barren woman and Ayọ̀ as a sterile man. Her arrival brought Ayọ̀ and Olúróunbí even closer to each other, and their love for one another continued to grow deeper and deeper every day. Ayọ̀, watching Olúróunbí dressing the two-month-old Olúfúnmi in a dress she had hand-sewn one morning, told his wife, "You know that my love for you is bursting at the seams, woman," sealing it with a kiss. "Thank you, my darling for making me a father."

"I am the one who should thank you and the Almighty God for making me a mother. Now, nobody can call me a barren woman that can never conceive nor give birth." Her pupils rolled around in the wetness of her tears as she responded to her husband. The infant's reaction seemed to indicate that she understood her parents. She made cooing sounds that penetrated to the core of her parents, striking a melodic chord in their hearts. They both started laughing. Olúfúnmi glanced wide-eyed into their faces in turns, exposing her toothless gums in a smile. And of course, they smothered her with kisses and cradling hugs against their maternal-paternal bodies.

Olúfúnmi, *ọmọ-pupa-apọ́n-bí-epo* (child-as-red-as-palm-oil), was growing up to be a delightful child with an infectious smile. She was the pride and joy not only of her parents but also of her grandparents and some of the town folks. She was very loving and friendly to everyone around her. At the age of four years old, her paternal grandfather, Bàbá Ayọ̀, spent most of his afternoons visiting Olúfúnmi and teaching her various skills and telling her stories of his valiant accomplishments on the battlefield. If he could not go to visit her, he instructed Olúróunbí to bring her over to the family compound. It soon became obvious that Olúfúnmi was Bàbá Ayọ̀'s new favorite grandchild. Màmá Ayọ̀ also recognized that Olúfúnmi had seized and claimed her heart. Almost every fortnight, she ordered new handwoven *aṣọ-òkè* fabrics, *àdìrẹ* tie-dye, batik brocade, and other fabrics and assigned a seamstress to make the latest style attires for Olúfúnmi. Also, Olúróunbí's parents did not lag in demonstrating their love for Olúfúnmi. Màmá Olúróunbí moved into her daughter's home to help with house chores, cooking and caring for the new infant as the customs of the land. As an experienced parent, a grandmother from either side of the family, but usually the wife's mother, stayed with new parents during the first few months of a newborn's life to assist with housework and teaching the new mother various parenting skills.

Ayọ̀ was often seen playing with her in front of their compound and sometimes carrying her on his shoulders through the town. Some people even criticized Ayọ̀ for being an indulgent father and for raising her like a boy, warning that he would spoil her rotten and would behave like a boy the way he was carrying on teaching her boy's stuff. Olúróunbí often expressed her disagreement with those opinions. She loved that Ayọ̀ was close to his daughter and had been teaching her a lot of things, especially about the science of hunting different animals, farming techniques, herbs, and roots. Olúfúnmi was fascinated about the diversity of animal species and of botanical sciences. She soaked up the information like a sponge. With every expressed amazement of knowledge shared, Ayọ̀ taught Olúfúnmi to glorify the Creator of these things. They made the pronouncements of the greatness of God as the best and unrivaled Creator.

Prior to Olúfúnmi's third birthday, Màmá Olúróunbí fell ill and passed away within a week. Bàbá Olúróunbí was devastated and unable to cope alone in their home, even though Olúróunbí, Ayọ̀, and Olúfúnmi visited as frequently as possible. Olúróunbí cooked three square meals for him every day without fail. He lasted less than a year before he joined his wife in eternal slumber. Olúróunbí was extremely saddened but also glad that her father was reunited with his wife and that his loneliness and grief had ended. She was aware that Olúfúnmi also missed her maternal grandparents. She felt sad that they would not see her grow further.

Chapter Seven
ÌKẸ AKẸJÚ - THE INDULGENCE

Every day was a new day of joyful parenting discoveries for Olúróunbí and Ayọ̀. Even though they did not have prior experience to compare Olúfúnmi to, except children in their families and in the neighborhood, they believed that she was the smartest, most loving, beautiful, and special child on Earth. Everything she did was exceptional and amazing. Ayọ̀ could not help indulging in granting her requests. During the daytime, she was Màmá's baby, but as soon as Ayọ̀ returned from work, she devoted her time and attention to her father. Olúróunbí would even joke that she was jealous of their adventurous games and explorations of the famous Ìlúgidi's botanical garden behind the houses. The father and daughter usually brought back unique fruits, leaves, roots, and herbs for Olúróunbí from their escapades. She served the fruits as snacks or part of a meal and used some of the leaves, roots, and herbs in her cooking or soaked them for medicinal àgbo mixtures. Ayọ̀ had been teaching Olúfúnmi their uses, so whenever they returned home, Olúfúnmi would show off her knowledge of nature's gifts to mankind and tell her mother their names and usefulness. Ayọ̀ would beam with pride at Olúfúnmi's brilliance and exceptional cognitive gift.

The crisp cold and dusty Harmattan season morning breeze greeted Ayọ̀ when he stepped out onto his front yard. He wore the tightly woven ankle length *sòkòtò* trousers and knee-length *bùbá* top that was thick enough to ward off the wind. Olúróunbí ensured that he had applied a thick layer of *òòrí* (shea butter) all over his body. She could not stand the ashy skin and dry lips that the Sahara Desert northeasterly trade wind adorned on people. Even though Ayọ̀ had bid his wife and daughter goodbye for the day inside the house, he found them trailing him outside. Olúfúnmi *Ọmọ-pupa-apọ́n-bí-epo* had a pout and a frown on her face. "Baba mi, why don't you stay home today? Please," she whined.

Ayọ̀ turned around, lifted his daughter, and climbed the four threshold steps back into the house. He held her at eye level. "My sweet daughter, I have to go to the farm because we are harvesting the maize, cassava, okra, and groundnut. At the same time, we must start preparing the seeds and roots for planting as soon as the two months' restful period for the farmland is completed. We also must store the harvested produce, you know. We have a lot of work these days, and I shouldn't leave our farm workers to do all the work."

Olúfúnmi nodded, understanding. However, she draped her arms around Ayọ̀'s neck and continued, "Okay, but can you just stay home with me and Mama mi today? The other farmers can do their part and you can do your part tomorrow. Please, Baba mi! Stay home, please!" her lashes repeatedly batting at him.

Olúróunbí, stepping back into the house, watched father and daughter bargaining. She observed a worried look on Olúfúnmi's countenance and a thoughtful look on Ayọ̀'s. It was obvious that Ayọ̀ was contemplating Olúfúnmi's entreaty. "Ayọ̀, my honorable husband, I think your daughter is right. You can tell Akin-lọmọ to oversee the work and supervise the other farmers for today. He will soon be here to trek to the farm with you as usual."

Ayọ̀ turned to his wife. "I am very tempted to stay home but there is so much to be organized and completed, and our farmers might think I'm just being a lazy man. I must be dependable. Besides, a lot of the traders are coming to buy their stock today for the market day tomorrow. *Ẹmá bìnu.*"

"Okay. How about going later in the day, Baba mi? We can eat breakfast together and then play my favorite game "*mo- níní, mo-níní, mo-níní, mo-níní, mo bárúgbó kan lódò.*" After that, you can go to the farm."

"Tell you what? I promise to come back early today. There is a proverb that our elders taught us that states, '*Àárò lojà (Early morning is the most profitable time in the market)*."

Olúfúnmi loved learning about the meaning of proverbs because she often heard grown people talk in proverbs that she did not understand. "What does that mean, Baba mi?"

"It means that the peak of trading is in the morning. You must get to the market early in order to get the best products at the right price. The traders will be arriving at the farm to buy our produce very early so that they can get to their customers early." As Ayò was explaining the proverb to Olúfúnmi, Akin-lomo sauntered into his compound, shouting his "*Ẹkáàrò o (Good morning)*" greetings. Ayò planted kisses on his daughter's forehead and cheeks before putting her back on the floor. He embraced his wife and bid them goodbye for the day.

Olúróunbí pulled Olúfúnmi closer and laid soothing hands around her shoulder, resting on her right hip. She noticed that she was tall for a five-year-old child and too intelligent for her age.

The trek to Ayọ's family farm was not as chatty as usual. Akin-lọmọ observed that his friend and employer seemed pensive this morning. He got tired of talking to himself, so he became quiet too. He struggled to keep up with Ayọ's faster pace and longer strides. He wondered what was bothering him. When they arrived at the farm, none of the hired farmers had arrived. They went into the *ahéré,* changed into their work clothes, retrieved their tools, and set about their work with minimal conversation.

Suddenly, Ayọ sighted a strange dark-grey snake racing toward him at an unexpected speed. He dexterously jumped sideways and immediately took off running. In an instant, Ayọ felt a large needle-like strike in his right calf that sent his lanky body to the leafy and twiggy dirt facedown. The most deafening sound emanated from his shuddering body. Ayọ, hands positioned flat on the ground, lifted his body, but his right leg felt like the heaviest log burdening his movement. He could not get up. Then, commanding his other leg, he flipped himself around and sat up, facing the snake. Its mouth, opened wide, revealed an impressive blue-black layer with hollow fangs at the front of its mouth. At that moment, Ayọ̀ felt the urgency to make a declaration. In rapid succession, just as rapid as the snake's multiple follow-up strikes of its fangs against Ayọ̀'s left thigh, Ayọ̀ screamed the scream of death as he started gasping for air. He heard his own voice calling out the names, Olúróunbí! Olúfúnmi! He felt a massive swelling inside his throat and an agonizing squeeze at the same time. Paralyzing stabs of pain shot through every part of his body. He thrust his torso up to a sitting position with the force of a laboring mother to push her burden out of the narrow pathway of life. Ayọ̀'s spine gave, seeming to have become jellified, and he fell back on to the ground. The snake, angered at the audacity of its prey to clasp his hands around its belly, speedily hacked up extra venom into its lethal teeth and landed another strike onto the flesh closest to it. The snake could feel Ayọ̀ loosening its grip.

Everything was happening so fast that he feared he would lose his voice and his life soon. "God be with you." He forced out the words as loud as he could manage. In response to the urgency he felt, he quickly followed up with a statement that pushed its way out of his fast, dissipating breath. "I pronounce my return to Thee, the only God." Halting, with the gurgle of death, he managed to continue uttering the words that he was determined to say. "You created me, and onto You, I am returning. You—you're the Lord of the universe and all therein." He struggled to say more, and his voice deserted him. The Black Mamba glared and hissed, waiting until Ayọ̀'s head fell backward and his body fully slumped onto the earth. Ayọ̀'s head hit the rough ground behind him. The snake hissed, uncurled itself, and quickly slithered up Ayọ̀'s chest onto his throat. The snake raised its head up as if it would strike Ayọ̀ again but instead scanned Ayọ̀ for any sign of life. Satisfied that there was none, it slithered its long body down Ayọ̀'s neck on to the leafy forest dirt and disappeared into oblivion.

Chapter Eight
ÌTÀN EJÒ MÀMÁ DÚDÚ - THE STORY OF THE MAMBA SNAKE

A family of Black Mamba snakes had made a home in a pit near the Savanna region in the southern hemisphere of the oldest continent on Earth and the birthplace of human beings, Africa. Several father and mother Black Mamba snakes had been rearing their offspring in this damp and mushy pit for an unknown number of years. They had enjoyed safety and security for so long that they had multiplied without any human or predator preying on them, except when some of them ventured out in search of feeding. The parents warned the babies to stay in the pit until maturity.

One day, a postpartum Màmá Black Mamba had just emerged from a nursery section of the pit after delivering several long eggs on the ground. Exhausted and perched, she slithered her way to a nearby pond after which she planned to hunt for nourishment to replenish her energy. A snake hunter who had been waiting around the pit, in a single motion, quickly and deftly clipped his work tool around Màmá Black Mamba's throat. The Velcro-covered steel tool clasped and tightened around her throat, preventing an escape. The hunter grabbed her wiggling and curling long body and deposited it into a bucket, released the clasp, and clanged the cover immediately over it. The hunter was aware of the speed and lethality of the snake, so he worked at the speed of lightning. The snake was so long that her curled-up body almost filled the *koroba* bucket to the top. The hunter left the scene immediately with his dangerous, precious catch. He could hear Màmá Black Mamba making dry, raspy growls, signaling her anger at having been captured.

Later that day, the snake hunter sold Màmá Black Mamba to a snake collector. Through trading, Màmá Black Mamba ended up in a strange land, very far away from her home. She was placed inside a cold cage made of iron and was barely fed. She felt isolated and mistreated with the way some rough human hands squeezed her head as they forced serum from her fangs into a container. They did these involuntary collections too often for her liking.

After several moons passed, one day, as dawn made its way to the area, removing the blanket of the night, the rough-handed man had just finished collecting some serum and was about to place Màmá Black Mamba into her solitary confinement when his fingers released her head a tad bit sooner. The snake did not miss the opportunity to quickly slip away. The man was not fast enough to grip her back and jumped aside, fearing an attack from her but instead saw her long body slither away in a zigzag pattern at top speed. The rough-handed man knew that he could not catch up with her, even if he was insane enough to go after her. The man ran inside to inform the medicine man of the escape.

It was during Màmá Black Mamba's frightful escape from captivity that she came upon two men who were striking the earth with tools. The one on her path raised his hoe above his head and was about to strike her. Màmá Black Mamba did what any threatened snake would do under the circumstances. She attacked before she was annihilated.

Chapter Nine
Ó FẸSẸ̀ FẸ – HE FLED

Ayọ̀'s farmer friend, Akin-lọmọ, who was employed by Ayọ̀, witnessed the humongous snake strike a deadly bite on Ayọ̀'s thigh. As he took flight, Akin-lọmọ saw the snake wrapped itself around the same leg ready to strike again. He did not wait around for his turn. His instinctive response of flight from fright showed the back of his bare head and his air-filled *dàṣíkí* to Ayọ̀, who had expected rescue from him. Although the pain excruciatingly overwhelmed Ayọ̀, he grabbed the snake at its midsection, pulled it, and tried to hurl it far away from him. Her slithery, slippery skin did not offer adequate friction for his aim to work. Màmá Black Mamba turned and twisted herself out of Ayọ̀'s grip then tightened her wrap. She raised her head in a combat position, opened her mouth, revealing an all-black lining, glared into Ayọ̀'s eyes, and with a victor's mock, swiftly dealt another strike at his other leg. Ayọ̀'s cry of a vanquished opponent roared through the forest, reaching the ears of the fleeing Akin-lọmọ.

Akin-lọmọ's scattering legs, with a single aim, continued to carry him in the opposite direction of the snake. He tore through shrubs, weaving through willowing branches, and ducking trees in the nick of time to prevent a head-on collision. Even though his energy was quickly depleting, he did not allow his uncoordinated legs to fail until the last breath in his lungs had dissipated. It was then that he grabbed at a tree in his path to break the velocity and acceleration of his legs. He clung to the tree, spun, and wrapped his arms around it. He gulped a series of breaths through his mouth and nostrils. His burning chest heaved up and down while his watery eyes had become red-hot charcoal. Akin-lọmọ hurriedly glanced behind him for the assailant he expected to be close on his tail. He did not see the snake. Again, his eyes darted around the area, and he became satisfied that there was no sign of any large snake slithering toward him. His burning throat started cooling off gradually, and the fast and loud drumming in his chest grew slower and quieter. He leaned on the tree and then started scanning the forest to figure out his whereabouts. He did not know how many acres of land he had covered, nor did he know whose land he was standing on. There were no pedestrian paths within his vision. *"Heeeeey! Heeeeey! Ejò oooo!* Anybody here? Please, is there any human being around here? Please, I need help *oooo!"* He shouted into the forest. All he heard momentarily were birds taking flight and small animals scurrying away. He yelled again, using the farmers' and hunters' howling sounds. He paused and listened intently until he finally heard the return call of a farmer. Akin-lọmọ repeated the call for help, directing the voice in the farmers' direction. The back-and-forth calls continued until his rescuer reached him where he was leaning against the tree trunk.

When Akin-lọmọ finally made it to his town and he narrated the event of the forest, he was taken to his house. It was then that his wife directed his attention to his scratched bruised legs and tattered cotton fabric trousers. Suddenly, he started feeling the pain from his forest-torn flesh.

Olúróunbí and Olúfúnmi were finishing up lunch in the eating section of the visitors' room when they heard loud voices shouting and wailing. Without pausing to wash their hands, they ran through the narrow corridor to the front yard where raucous was unfolding. Amid a group of people, they saw Akin-lọmọ throw himself on the ground, wailing and spouting incomprehensible phrases.

"Where did this happen?" Olúróunbí heard someone asking Akin-lọmọ.

"Stop wailing so we can understand what you're saying, Akin-lọmọ," shouted another man.

Olúróunbí and Olúfúnmi descended from the house steps and rushed to where Akin-lọmọ was scattered.

"What's going on? Where's my husband?" her voice sounded strained and worried.

Akin-lọmọ glanced up at Olúróunbí and started to wail again and louder.

"Stop crying and tell me what happened, please."

Akin-lomo swallowed as if he were swallowing a large lump of *fùfú (cassava meal)* and commenced to narrate the event of the morning leading to the strange snake attack and how he heard and saw Ayọ̀ succumb to death from the infliction of the snake. In order not to seem like a coward, he embellished his narration by adding that he tried to rescue Ayọ̀ but that the snake was a strange one, and its movement was unpredictable. He described the excessive length of the slim snake, the blackness of its mouth, and the immediate effect of its quick multiple strikes before he ran for his life.

During his narration, Olúróunbí reacted as if the snake were striking her at the same time. Hysteria took a grip of her while little Olúfúnmi began to stomp her feet on the ground and scream. Mother and daughter were in a state of indescribable grief and shock. At some point, Olúróunbí lost her stand and was rolling on the ground. Olúfúnmi seemed more alarmed at her mother's display of near insanity than at the tragedy of her father's death. One of their neighbors took over the comforting of Olúfúnmi. She lowered her body to a kneeling position in order to match Olúfúnmi's height. She wrapped her arms around her body and held her tight. Olúfúnmi sobbed into her neighbor's shoulder as she patted her on the back as if lulling a baby to sleep.

The tragic news of Ayọ̀'s accidental death soon reached his parents, the King's palace, and the entire town. It spread like a dry-season forest fire. Without much delay, a search team was mobilized that followed Akin-lọmọ to the site of the incident. Based on his account, it was not clear whether Ayọ̀ was dead or alive. The search party was charged with finding Ayọ̀ or his corpse. Armed with hunter's guns, axes, cutlasses *gbóńgbó, àpólà (heavy sticks)*, and other weapons, they marched to Ayọ̀'s farm. When they got to the spot where Akin-lọmọ pointed out to them, Ayọ̀ could not be found. Akin-lọmọ turned in every direction, scratching his head and rubbing his eyes intermittently. He pointed repeatedly at the spot, walked a few paces up and down, right and left, blabbing incomplete phrases and looking at the escorts until he started to tremble fearfully. "I think the snake must have been an evil spirit. After biting Ayọ̀, it must have taken his body with it," he stated almost in a whisper lest the suspected evil spirit heard him and came back to grab him too.

"What nonsense are you saying?" asked Ayọ̀'s closest friend, Rótìmí who had rushed to his house as soon as he heard about the incident.

Akin-lọmọ stared at him. His face was contorted with terror and confusion. "I mean, how would you explain the disappearance of Ayọ̀? I saw him bitten by a snake this morning. Didn't I?" he asked, perturbed.

"Well then, what could've happened to him?" Rótìmí shrugged in confusion, looking at others who appeared as confused as he was.

They continued sweeping the surrounding area, shouting his name as loud as possible in the hope that the winds would carry it through the farmlands and the forest to wherever he might be in a radius of *ibùsọ̀ méjì*, or two miles, without a trace of Ayọ̀, except for his cap and the imprint of his body on the scattered plantation dirt during the battle with the snake. There were no traces of a dragged body or footprints anywhere on the ground. "Did Ayọ̀ evaporate mysteriously or did somebody rescue and take him away?" asked a stocky man in a knee-length *Kẹ̀mbẹ̀* and matching *bùbá top,* whose watering eyes seemed dilated with fear. After repeated roundabouts of the search area, the exhausted party had lost hope of solving the mystery of Ayọ̀—dead or alive. They dragged their weary feet back to Ìlúgidi, searching everywhere and shouting Ayọ̀'s name along the route. The search continued beyond the combed areas into neighboring villages and farmlands the following day and more days after that. Olúróunbí and Olúfúnmi followed the party on some of them, all to no avail. Eventually, a funeral ceremony in the absence of his corpse was arranged against Olúróunbí's approval.

Chapter Ten
ÀTÙPÀ TI KÚ – THE EXTINGUISHED LANTERN

The light seemed to have been snuffed out from Olúróunbí's life with the death of her husband. She felt that her life had been turned upside down and spilled into the gutter that ran its filth into the sewer. These days, her mind was perpetually in a state of confusion and unfathomable misery. She could barely tell the difference between wakefulness and sleep. Her sleep was crowded with a series of nightmares that did not make sense. And there was the case of her daughter and her state of being. Olúróunbí did not know how to console her grief-stricken daughter. Olúfúnmi kept on asking for her father. All the answers given were not acceptable to Olúfúnmi.

One day, she learned that Bàbá Ayọ̀ was blaming her for the death of Ayọ̀. Olúróunbí had heard that Bàbá Ayọ̀ had been raining curses and damnation on her for sending his son to his death. She heard that he had said, "First, she delayed Ayọ̀ for many years without giving him a child. When she finally decided to birth him a child, she failed as a good wife to give Ayọ̀ a son to fulfill the destiny of the Àjàní's posterity and the town's glory. Then she sent him to his death in spite Olúfúnmi's warning not to let Ayọ̀ go to the farm on that fateful day."

One day, Olúróunbí summoned up all the energy and courage she had left and went to visit her in-laws to clear herself of the rumors and to attempt to grieve their loss together, as a family. When she arrived at the Àjàní compound, she observed that some of the women avoided her and hurried into their respective quarters. The men greeted her without warmth and pretended to busy themselves with insignificant tasks. Some were examining the patterns on their palms and their fingernails; others pretended to be engaged in deep conversations with one another while spying at her from the corners of their eyes. Olúróunbí sighed heavily and proceeded to knock on the opened door of her in-law's house.

"Enter," announced the voice of Màmá Ayọ̀.

Olúróunbí pulled the curtain aside to reveal herself. She beheld Bàbá Ayọ̀ sitting on a recliner. His knitted brows showed more lines than usual, and the pupils of his protruding eyes seemed two shades darker than the darkest brown eye color. His lips were squeezed into a tight knot as if forbidden to open his mouth forever. The jaws on both sides of his face engaged in continuous squeezing and relaxing until he saw the door curtain drawn open. When Bàbá Ayọ̀'s eye rested on Olúróunbí, the browns crept even closer into an impossible frown. His darkened eyes grew darker and fiery. He slowly brought his body to a sitting position without bothering to right the recliner.

"If your child was a boy, I would have taken him from you to raise as the true heir of the family but since the child is female, you can keep her and raise her as you like. She's of no use to securing and preserving the Sovereignty of Ìlúgidi Town, anyway," Bàbá Ayọ̀ spat while Màmá Ayọ̀'s eyes remained glued to the floor near her feet.

Hot tears quickly filled up the well of Olúróunbí's eyes and pain filled up in the gut of her stomach; her quivering lips could not utter the words that had gathered on her tongue. Her chest felt like reddened coal was being thrust in with every utterance that her father-in-law hurled at her. "But, Bàbá mi, why—?"

"Don't call me your father! I'm not your father. You have no father; your father is dead!" His voice resembled the rainy season's booming thunder.

Màmá Ayọ̀ twisted uneasily in her seat but did not make any sound, she was too grief-stricken to defend Olúróunbí. She brought her hands up and held her head's temples as if trying to prevent an explosion.

Bàbá Ayọ̀ continued to unleash ferocious utterings and curses at Olúróunbí. She remained respectfully on her knees with arms folded over her midsection. "You will be wretched all your life. You have no father, no mother, and now you have caused your husband's death," he insisted.

Olúróunbí lifted her head and looked straight at her father-in-law. "*Ẹ jọ̀*, Baba mi, with all due respect," ignoring his command not to address him as her father, she asked, "How did I cause the death of my husband?"

He regarded her with disdain. "You sent him to his death when your daughter told him not to go to the farm that day. Or did she not?"

"Yes, Baba mi, she did." Her head dropped to her chest. She sighed. "But—"

"But what? If you're a good wife, you'd have prevented him from venturing out that day. You should have supported your daughter and insisted that he must not go farming. Besides, I have always told Ayọ̀ not to relegate himself to a mere farmer. He's a great warrior and a skilled hunter from a prestigious family. Why should he engage in the menial work of farming when he could just employ farmers to do the work? And that's something you should also have ensured. This would not have happened if you were a good and smart wife.

The inner wound in Olúróunbí's heart that was attempting to healing was ripped open afresh by her father-in-law. She agreed with some of the things he spewed at her. *Yes, I should have insisted that he stayed home that terrible day. He might have listened, and he would have been alive today.* Olúróunbí had been blaming herself ever since the incidence. She was unable to forgive herself.

Olúróunbí begged her father-in-law for forgiveness, but Bàbá Ayọ̀ declined. He also made a declaration for eternal enmity with Olúróunbí and forbade her from ever stepping foot in the Àjàní compound. "*Mo kọ̀ ré tọmọ-tọmọ;* you're divorced along with your child from now on. Don't bring your daughter to my house; she is no longer a member of this household. If you see me anywhere, don't greet or open your mouth to say a word to me or any member of my family. If you do, you will be damned forever." With that, he rose, turned and strode towards a curtained door at the left of the recliner that led to an inner chamber. Màmá Ayọ̀ mimicked her husband's motion and was fast at his heels. Bàbá Ayọ̀ pulled the curtain aside and was about to enter through the door when he heard a resounding voice.

"Stop right there, sir!" the voice commanded.

Olúróunbí peeled her knees from the floor as if they were oak tree trunks and stood up. She took a couple of steps towards Ayọ̀'s parents who had obeyed despite themselves.

Bàbá Ayọ̀'s eyes widened in disbelief; Màmá Ayọ̀'s jaw fell as if there were no bones or muscles to keep them from hitting the floor.

"What did you say, woman?" an incredulous tone sounded in Bàbá Ayọ̀'s voice.

"Well sir, you spoke, and you should wait for a response, sir."

"You dare respond to me?"

"Yes, sir!" Without waiting for him to respond, Olúróunbí started speaking quickly and deliberately. "First of all, I need to inform you that you're not God. You're a mere man, just like your wife and I are just mere women. Mere mortals." She observed that Màmá Ayọ̀'s head rose up, jaw dropped, mouth agape, eyes widened in a stare. Olúróunbí continued. "You're a cruel man. You've been mean to me throughout most of my marriage to your son. Ever since the fifth moon passed and I wasn't pregnant, I had observed your negative attitude towards me. You started threatening to get another wife for my husband to give him children. You blamed me for everything, even things that I have no control over. When we gave birth to Olufunmi, you rejected her because she was not a boy. Now, my husband died tragically, and you blame me for that too. You're a wicked man, indeed..."

"OLÚRÓUNBÍ, HAVE YOU LOST YOUR SENSES?!" Bàbá shouted, his voice quivering with rage.

"No sir," she raised her voice, squared her shoulders and lifted her chin a notch higher. "I haven't lost my mind. I just need to let you know that you have lost the honor and respect that I had previously accorded you. You were my father-in-law until you disowned your grand-daughter and rejected me as your daughter-in-law. Therefore, you're a nonentity from now on. You're now just a mere man as far as I'm concerned."

"Get out of my house, stupid woman! Right now! Get out!" His chest heaved up and down; his protruding eyes bulged so much that the lids were tucked out of sight; finger pointed menacingly at the door. He started at her like an enraged bull approaching a tormenting matador.

Olúróunbí stood her ground and glared daringly at him. He slackened his pace but maintained his threatening voice. At that point, Màmá Ayọ̀ tugged at her husband's *agbádá* (men's flowy garment), but she could not find her voice to utter her thoughts.

Olurounbi replied where her feet remained planted. "I will leave your house, but before I go, I want to tell you that I will not be wretched. I will not die a wretched death. Even though, my parents have gone back to where you too shall go one day. I have God. And since God will never die; He will take care of me and my child. We shall not be wretched as you wish. Remember that what you wish for others might become your portion." She then turned around and walked gingerly out, leaving behind the stupefied couple.

Olúróunbí stormed out of the Àjàní's compound towards her joyless home, tears gushing out of her eyes streaming down her cheeks onto the corners of her mouth and down her chin to her neck and soaking the neckline of her *bùbá (top)*. Olúróunbí marched through the streets, oblivious of questioning and concerned countenances staring at her. Some people even addressed her, but she hurried along without any response. It was not until she reached her house that she realized how leaden her feet felt. She had to exert tremendous effort to drag them up the steps into the corridor and to her bed where she immediately slept.

Chapter Eleven
ÌGBÀ RERÉ TI DÉ – CHANGE IN FORTUNE

Olúfúnmi and Olúróunbí remained devastated by Ayọ̀'s sudden death.

They felt lost in the world without him. The little girl seemed to have lost her laughter, and her mother moved around as if her legs were too heavy to carry her body.

Olúróunbí and Olúfúnmi's relatives and some of the townspeople tried to console them with donations and kind words. The donations helped with some of the living expenses. After a while, little by little, the gifts and donations stopped coming, and all the money was depleted. Olúróunbí, who had been an exclusive home-keeper matriarch and wife when her husband was alive, had to go out and find a way to make a living.

Olúróunbí eventually purchased some goods and started selling at a market some many miles away, called the Alátùnṣe Market.

Usually, Olúróunbí and her daughter, Olúfúnmi set out on foot before the break of dawn to the market, and they did not return until the sun had gone down. Both mother and daughter's trek to and from the market and the trading hard work were so exhausting that they were too tired to have their supper sometimes. In addition to this, their sales were usually poor. They barely made enough money to eat twice a day.

People came from far and near to trade at the Alátùnṣe Market, so the competition was fierce. Many of the traders were thriving in their various businesses, but Olúróunbí continued to have a hard time selling her wares. Buyers passed her stall without checking out her goods but bought from the stalls on either side of her. Olúfúnmi helped her mother advertise by calling out bargain prices of the wares, yet only a few purchased anything.

Olúróunbí was beginning to believe that there was a curse on her luck; or that Baba Ayo may be right and that she would be wretched and poor forever. During the daily trek to and from the market, Olurounbi sang soulful, sorrowful songs of her woes. Tears easily found their way out of her eyes these days. One day, she cried harder when she heard Olúfúnmi singing along:

Oro ma re‑e‑e‑e, ara adugbo

Nígbà mo mí lọ sójà, ojú ń ro mi

(As I head for the market, I am full of apprehension)

Ìgbà mo mí ń padà bọ̀

(On my return)

Jẹ́kí ọ̀rọ̀ mi má dayọ̀

(I pray that I will rejoice)

Ọba *rere mába ayọ̀ mi je fun mi*

(Oh, Good Lord, let not misery be my lot)

Ọba *rere mágbọ̀rọ́ ẹkún bámi*

(Oh, Good Lord, let me not have cause to weep)

Then, one day, Olúróunbí heard about a shortcut through Ìdí Ìrókò to the Alátùnṣe Market, and she decided to take it. She and her daughter set out as the day was about to break. They walked through a dense forest pathway and soon came upon a large Ìrókò tree stationed at the entrance of Ìdí Ìrókò town. Olúróunbí and Olúfúnmi beheld a small group of people gathered at the foot of the tree, seeming to be talking to the tree. It towered over all the other trees in the forest. Its trunk was majestically enormous. The base branched out all around and extended several feet away, serving as a resting platform to the left, and a couple of large bricks lay on the right. Tentatively, they moved closer to the crowd and strained to hear what was being said.

"Oh, great Ìrókò tree! King of all trees! The oracle spirits!" started a man carrying two big sacks of tools. "I am heading to the Alátùnṣe Market to sell my wares; please grant me the gift of trade success (Aje), and I will be very grateful to you." He clasped both hands beseechingly.

Olúróunbí and Olúfúnmi watched curiously. Suddenly, a deep voice sounded from the bowel of the tree, frightening them both. "And what will you give me in return, if I grant your request?" asked the voice.

The man with the tool wares replied without fear or apprehension. "Great Ìrókò Spirit, I vow to give you a fat and robust sheep for your pleasure if you grant my request to sell all my wares with good profit."

"You shall succeed and make a very good profit, but you must not forget your promise," Iroko Oracle announced. "You must bring my fat and robust sheep on your way back from Alátùnṣe Market, or else."

The man with the tool wares picked up his two sacks, reiterating his promise, and scampered happily along.

Then another man took his place and presented his request the same way the man with the tool wares did and the same dialogue was exchanged between him and the Ìrókò tree. After promising to bring a strong and tall goat in exchange for a successful market day, he also went along happily praising the tree. Then a woman with a tall tower of cosmetic, herbs, health and beauty goods *(àtíkè, òòrí, osùn, ọṣẹ dúdú, àdí-àgbọn, konkon)* balanced on her head presented her request the same way. The Ìrókò tree assured her that the tower of cosmetics would be flat and empty. Her pouch would be filled with money by the end of the market day. So, she vowed to give the Ìrókò tree a fat, plump turkey in return.

Olúróunbí and Olúfúnmi were stunned as they watched the incredible spectacle until all the traders were gone by their businesses. The Ìrókò tree bellowed out, "Woman with the beautiful red child! Do you have a request for the King of the Woods, or did you just come to stare with saliva drooling from your mouth?"

Both mother and child uprooted their feet and jumped backward, ready to run.

"Ha ha ha, you are so timid," roared the tree with laughter. "See how you both jumped abruptly like monkeys."

Olúróunbí composed herself and stepped closer to the Ìrókò tree. "Oh you! great king of the woods," she started tentatively, "I am a petty trader, and I hardly make sales at the market every day. So, I pray that you can grant my request as you promised the people before me."

The Ìrókò tree sighed and asked, "If I give you the gift of a profitable market day, what would you offer me in return, oh woman with the beautiful red-skinned child?"

Olúróunbí glanced around helplessly and looked at her daughter. "Oh, great Ìrókò tree, I have nothing to offer you. I am a poor widow with nothing of value to offer you."

"Everyone has something of value to offer," the Ìrókò tree countered. "If you want the great king of the woods to grant you success, you must be willing to sacrifice to me in return."

"I shall gladly sacrifice to you, great king of the woods if I have the means. But I swear to you, I do not have anything of value to offer you, great Ìrókò tree."

"But you do, ye woman with the beautiful red-complexioned child."

"Oh, great Ìrókò tree, after my husband passed away, all that he left is gone. I have nothing except my only child, Olúfúnmi," Olúróunbí surmised, pulling Olúfúnmi closer to her bosom.

The Ìrókò tree called out, "That is what I request from you as a sacrifice. I will give you seven moons during which you will become the most successful trader in the market and the richest person in the land; then you have to bring your child with skin as red as palm oil to me."

Olúróunbí made a sudden gesture of retreat, screaming, "Olúfúnmi! *Come!* Let's go our way! This is a mad request!" She pulled frantically at Olúfúnmi, who seemed to be nailed to the ground.

The mother pulled at her child and started to run away. The Ìrókò tree spoke soothingly, "Olúróunbí, come back. The great Ìrókò spirit shall make you the richest woman in the land if you accept my proposal. You can own anything and even get a new husband who can give you many children. Just give me this child, Olúfúnmi."

Olúróunbí was surprised that the Ìrókò tree knew her and her daughter's name. She reckoned that the spirit of the Ìrókò tree was indeed a powerful oracle. She found herself in a dilemma. She needed to get herself and her daughter out of the wretchedness that fate had dealt them. She contemplated her current dilemma. Her father-in-law had ostracized them from his household and forbade Màmá Ayọ̀ from interacting with them. Her parents had passed away within a year of each other. Being an only child, Olúróunbí had no siblings who could come to her aid. Rótìmí, Ayọ̀'s bosom friend, was struggling with a chronic health condition that prevented his ability to ambulate, and Rótìmí's wife had despised Olúróunbí since they were young girls in the town of Ìlúgidi. Most of the people in town no longer associated with Olúróunbí because of their belief in the rumor that she was responsible for her husband's death. And those who still befriended her and Olúfúnmi could not continue to help financially. She had sold most of her tangible belongings and valuables for sustenance. Besides, the tree could not take her child, a human, from her. She turned and faced the Ìrókò tree again. "In how many moons did you say

I will become the richest person in the land, oh great king of the woods?" she asked.

"In—seven—moons," it replied. "After that, you must bring me my offering."

"If it is so, I shall fulfill my promise," she said.

"Make the declaration that you will bring me your daughter, Olúfúnmi *ọmọ-pupa-apọ́n-bí-epo* on the seventh moon."

"If you make me rich so that my daughter and I will never be wretched again, I will give her to the Ìrókò tree after seven moons," Olúróunbí declared. Afterward, she thought she heard a whistling of the wind and a rustling of leaves atop the skyscraper Ìrókò tree. She dismissed the thought and returned her attention to the tree.

"Seven moons it is. The covenant is sealed," Ìrókò pronounced.

"Seven moons it is," Olúróunbí accepted. Gathering her scanty wares, she pulled Olúfúnmi by the arm and hastened along toward the Alátùnṣe Market. As they neared the market, Olúróunbí realized that her daughter had been in a pensive mood ever since they left the Ìrókò tree.

She placed an arm around her and hugged her. "Are you worried because of my promise to the Ìrókò tree?" she asked her daughter.

"Yes, Màmá. You promised to give me away to the Ìrókò tree," she demanded, looking up into her mother's face. "Why, Màmá? You want to sacrifice me to be the richest woman in the land?" she asked, trying to fight tears from streaming down her eyes. "Does it mean I will be living with the tree in that forest?"

"No, My dear daughter! No. I will never sacrifice you for money or anything in this world."

"Then, why did you agree to give me to him so he could make you rich?" The tears gushed out of Olúfúnmi's eyes, and her chest started heaving up and down. Olúróunbí could see the confusion on her furrowed face and heard the panic in her quivering voice.

"Listen, my daughter. I didn't mean what I said to Ìrókò. Besides, I didn't think you'd believe such nonsense. How can the tree have the power to make me the richest woman in the land? It's not possible because he is not God, only God can do it.

Ìrókò is just a spirit-inhabited tree that can talk to humans. Besides, I will never give you away for anything in the world. You're my only child and the most beautiful child in the land," Olúróunbí assured her daughter and dried her wet face with the tip of her wrapper. She erased her worries with her reassuring smile.

At the Alátùnṣe Market, Olúróunbí set up her wares on her stall the usual way. Before she was done setting up, she noticed that a group of buyers had clustered across from her stall, waiting impatiently. As she was about to sit behind the stall and hope some of the customers would buy from her, the cluster of people rushed toward her and cleared her scanty stall within minutes without haggling for a price reduction.

"Trader! How can you bring such a small number of items to the market?" blurted one of the annoyed customers who did not find anything left to purchase. "I didn't get any of my usual provision today, and you know that I've been waiting since—"

"I'm so sorry, sir. I will bring more goods tomorrow if you don't mind," pleaded Olúróunbí, trying to compose herself from the shock of what had just happened to her.

Olúróunbí's eyes widened, lifting her brows a notch while the brownness seemed to glow a bit more than it had since the absence of her husband. She glanced at her daughter; whose face seemed to reflect her own disbelief. Mother and daughter, with upturned open mouths, looked at each other and at their stall. Olúfúnmi pointed at their empty stall as if to confirm if her mother realized that they were completely sold out of their goods. Olúróunbí glanced around and noticed that her fellow traders were also staring at her stall. While Olúróunbí and her daughter were preoccupied with attending to all the demanding customers, they had been staring at them in astonished disbelief. They had never seen anything like this in any market. Everyone was aware that some sellers had the gift of *owó ajé* (profitable hand) more than others, but they had never seen or heard of anyone who controlled the market like this. Olúróunbí's high cheekbones enthroned her face with the spread of her lips just as her daughter giggled nonstop. Olúróunbí heard herself humming a praise song.

By and by, a seller to the left of her stall, called Màmá Rómoké, sauntered closer, "Ehem-ehem, can you," she started tentatively, "help me sell some of my wares and we can share the profit?"

Olúróunbí regarded the trader for a moment as if she did not comprehend the request. She glanced at her daughter, her emptied stall, the cluster of anxious customers, the other marketers who were staring at her, and then back at Màmá. She turned the thought around in her mind only briefly, rationalizing that the market day had just started, and since she had nothing else to sell, she might as well make more money. So, she accepted the offer. She accepted and helped Màmá Rọ̀mọ́ké in transferring the basins of beans, the highly nutritious mineral and fiberfill rice, *ìrẹsì Ọ̀fadà* and the easily digestible fluffy needle-thin rice that melts in the mouth, *ìrẹsì alábẹ́rẹ́* onto her stand. As soon as the merchandising of the goods was dexterously completed, customers surged forward, shouting out orders.

Olúróunbí conducted the transactions while Olúfúnmi and Màmá Rọ̀mọké handled the packaging and customer services. Within a short time, all the goods had been sold. Màmá Rọ̀mọké threw her body on Olúróunbí in a tight grateful embrace. Olúfúnmi broke out in joyful singing and dancing. At that moment, the seller on the other side of Olúróunbí's stall followed Màmá Rọ́mọké's pathway. She made a similar offer, and all her *èlùbọ́ (yam flour) and gari (fine cassava grains)* were also sold within a short time. Before long, the news had spread throughout the market that God had made Olúróunbí's stall the abode for *aje,* ensuring profitable trade. Every seller came and invited Olúróunbí to their stands with offers to sell their goods in exchange profit-sharing. At the end of the day, Alátùnṣe Market was practically empty of goods. The traders were very happy, especially with Olúróunbí.

The following market day, some of the surrounding towns and villages had heard about Alátùnṣe Market and the woman with *ọwọ́ ajé* (hand of good fortune) so they brought their goods and handed them to Olúróunbí who then distributed to the retail traders at the market. By the third market day, Olúróunbí was established as the sole distributor of all goods that came to Alátùnṣe Market, and everybody went home happy.

The news had spread through the entire town. Olúróunbí had risen from grass to grace. Some of her foes had turned to friends, and the Ọba of Ìlúgidi town summoned her to his palace for commendation as one of the most honored members of the town. In an elaborate festivity, he crowned her as the revered *Ìyálọ́jà* (Market Leader) of Alátùnṣe Market.

Some of the women who had been Olúróunbí's adversaries began to seek her friendship. Men of diverse socioeconomic statuses lined up with avowals of everlasting love and marriage. Olúróunbí recognized and remembered that a lot of these people were engaged in labeling her a "barren woman," a "husband killer," and other things that she did not even want to think of. In a non-malicious way, she used the opportunities to remind them of their ill-treatment of her and how they believed the rumor that she was responsible for her late husband's death. Some of the shamed faces recoiled away while some apologized for their behaviors.

Olúfúnmi also was propelled into stardom among her peers. Both boys and girls of Ìlúgidi crowded her like bees hovering around their hives. A new clique had formed to rival the existing cliques. Within a short time, Olúfúnmi's friends had outnumbered others. Competition became fierce among her followers as they vied to be Olúfúnmi's best friend. Olúfúnmi's humility was demonstrated when the competition almost got out of hand one day during their playtime in a nearby sandy clearing between Bọlá and Bíọlá. "Everyone knows that I'm Fúnmi's best friend. Why are you now trying to pretend to be her best friend?" Bíọlá thrust her tiny frame at Bọlá while waving her tiny fingers wildly at her face.

Bọlá thrust her thicker frame back at Bíọlá and mimicked the wild hand-waving. "Who do you think you are? Do you think you can just appoint yourself as Fúnmi's best friend? What gives you the right?"

"She's my best friend because I've been her friend ever since we were little girls. We live next door to each other and Màmá mi and Màmá Fúnmi are also friends," retorted Bíọlá triumphantly. She observed that most of the other friends agreed with her with the nods of their heads.

Feeling somewhat defeated, Bọlá turned to Olúfúnmi with pursed lips and drooping eyelids. "Am I not your best friend?" she asked as more of a plea than a question. "You know that I like you most and I know you like me the most, right?" She twisted her body toward Bíọlá, rolled her eyes and did a meschew hissing at her.

Before Olúfúnmi had a chance to respond, Bíọlá interjected with her own meschew hissing from the corner teeth, drawing in more air for competitive elongation. She then planted herself in front of Olúfúnmi, intentionally blocking Bọlá off from view. "Fúnmi, you remember that this girl used to say bad things about you and your Màmá? She used to call you a spoiled rotten girl. Remember? And that your Màmá —"

Olúfúnmi raised her hand up to cut Bíọlá off. "We don't need to fight … Let's not argue," she pleaded in a soft voice. "We're all friends. You're all my best friends and I like all of you the same," teeth exposed, lips curled up and eyes gleaming, she coaxed.

After a brief awkward silence, "Let's play the *Tẹntẹ́* game and show the boys that we're not fighting," Olúfúnmi suggested and rolled her eyes at the group of boys who were part of Olúfúnmi's clique. They had been snickering throughout the feud between Bíọlá and Bọlá. Olúfúnmi started the handclapping in rhythm with foot-tapping on the dusty playground. The girls divided into two groups and lined up behind Olúfúnmi and Bọlá who had selected herself as the leader of the opposing group. Bíọlá placed herself behind Olúfúnmi. *"Tẹntẹ́…tẹntẹ́ … tẹntẹ́ …ìwo…ìwo…ìwo kẹ̀,"* they sang at each round. Some of the boys decided to help keep the scores of the *tẹntẹ́* while others occupied their time chasing after and kicking a thick rubber ball, targeting a post between two parallel trees hemming the bush.

On the day of the coronation, Olúróunbí was given horses to transport her and daughter to the market every day. Her wardrobe and that of Olúfúnmi had transformed from tattered *Ankara* cotton print to silky thread handwoven *aṣọ-òkè* of the best quality by the best weaver. More children of Ìlúgidi had started competing to befriend Olúfúnmi, and more eligible men vied for Olúróunbí's attention.

On the other hand, Bàbá Ayọ̀'s negative feelings for Olúróunbí rose to a higher level, bordering on lethal hatred. He had forbidden her and Olúfúnmi from entering his compound despite entreaties from Ọba Ìlúgidi and other well-meaning members of the community. He maintained his decision and forbade his wife and other family members from interacting with them. Olúróunbí's newfound success truly angered him to his core.

At the Alátùnṣe Market, Olúróunbí set up her wares on her stall the usual way. Before she was done setting up, she noticed that a group of buyers had clustered across from her stall, waiting impatiently. As she was about to sit behind the stall and hope some of the customers would patronize her, the cluster of people rushed toward her and cleared her scanty stall within minutes without haggling for a price reduction.

"Trader! How can you bring such a small number of items to the market?" blurted one of the annoyed customers who did not find anything left to purchase. "I didn't get any of my usual provision today, and you know that I've been waiting since—"

"I'm so sorry, sir. I will bring more goods tomorrow if you don't mind," pleaded Olúróunbí, trying to compose herself from the shock of what had just happened to her.

Olúróunbí's eyes widened, lifting her brows a notch while the brownness seemed to glow a bit more than it had since the absence of her husband.

She glanced at her daughter; whose face seemed to reflect her own disbelief. Mother and daughter, with upturned open mouths, looked at each other and at their stall. Olúfúnmi pointed at their empty stall as if to confirm if her mother realized that they were completely sold out of their goods. Olúróunbí glanced around and noticed that her fellow traders were also staring at her stall. While Olúróunbí and her daughter were preoccupied with attending to all the demanding customers, they had been staring at them in astonished disbelief. They had never seen anything like this in any market. Everyone was aware that some sellers had the gift of *ọwọ́ ajé* (profitable hand) more than others, but they had never seen or heard of anyone who controlled the market like this. Olúróunbí's high cheekbones enthroned her face with the spread of her lips just as her daughter giggled nonstop. Olúróunbí heard herself humming a praise song.

By and by, a seller to the left of her stall, called Màmá Rọ́mọké, sauntered closer, "Ehem-

ehem, can you," she started tentatively, "help me sell some of my wares and we can share the profit?"

Olúróunbí regarded the trader for a moment as if she did not comprehend the request. She glanced at her daughter, her emptied stall, the cluster of anxious customers, the other marketers who were staring at her, and then back at Màmá. She turned the thought around in her mind only briefly, rationalizing that the market day had just started, and since she had nothing else to sell, she might as well make more money. So, she accepted the offer. She accepted and helped Màmá Rómoké in transferring the basins of beans, the highly nutritious mineral and fiberfill rice, *ìresì Ọ̀fadà* and the easily digestible fluffy needle-thin rice that melts in the mouth, *ìresì alábẹ́rẹ́* onto her stand. As soon as the merchandising of the goods were dexterously completed, customers surged forward, shouting out their orders.

Olúróunbí conducted the transactions while Olúfúnmi and Màmá Rọmọké handled the packaging and customer services. Within a short time, all the goods had been sold. Màmá Rọmọké threw her body on Olúróunbí in a tight grateful embrace. Olúfúnmi broke out in a joyful singing and dancing. At that moment, the seller on the other side of Olúróunbí's stall followed Màmá Rọmọké's pathway. She made a similar offer, and all her *èlùbọ́ (yam flour fùfú) and gari (fine cassava grains)* were also sold within a short time. Before long, the news had spread throughout the market that God had made Olúróunbí's stall the abode for *aje,* ensuring profitable trade. So, every seller came and invited Olúróunbí to their stands with offers to sell their goods in exchange profit-sharing. At the end of the day, Alátùnṣe Market was practically empty of goods. The traders were very happy, especially with Olúróunbí.

The following market day, some of the surrounding towns and villages had heard about Alátùnṣe Market and the woman with *ọwọ́ ajé* (hand of good fortune) so they brought their goods and handed them to Olúróunbí who then distributed to the retail traders at the market. By the third market day, Olúróunbí was established as the sole distributor of all goods that came to Alátùnṣe Market, and everybody went home happy.

The news had spread through the entire town. Olúróunbí had risen from grass to grace. Some of her foes had turned to friends, and the Ọba of Ìlúgidi town summoned her to his palace for commendation as one of the most honored members of the town. In an elaborate festivity, he crowned her as the revered *Ìyálọ́jà* (Market Leader) Alátùnṣe Market.

Some of the women who had been Olúróunbí's adversaries began to covet her friendship. Men of diverse socioeconomic statuses lined up with avowals of everlasting love and marriage. Olúróunbí recognized and remembered that a lot of these people were engaged in labeling her a "barren woman," a "husband killer," and other things that she did not even want to think of. In a non-malicious way, she used the opportunities to remind them of their ill-treatment of her and how they believed the rumor that she was responsible for her late husband's death. Some of the shamed faces recoiled away while some apologized for their behaviors.

Olúfúnmi also was propelled into stardom among her peers. Both boys and girls of Ìlúgidi crowded her like bees hovering around their hives. A new clique had formed to rival the existing cliques. Within a short time, Olúfúnmi's friends had outnumbered others. Competition became fierce among her followers as they vied to be her best friend. Olúfúnmi's humility was demonstrated when the competition almost got out of hand one day during their playtime in a nearby sandy clearing between Bola and Bíọlá. "Everyone knows that I'm Fúnmi's best friend. Why are you now trying to pretend to be her best friend?" Bíọlá thrust her tiny frame at Bola while waving her tiny fingers wildly at her face.

Bola thrust her thicker frame back at Bíọlá and mimicked the wild hand-waving. "Who do you think you are? You think you can just appoint yourself as Fúnmi's best friend? What makes you her best friend?"

"She's my best friend because I've been her friend ever since we were little girls. We live next door to each other and Màmá mi and Màmá Fúnmi are also friends," retorted Bíọlá triumphantly. She observed that most of the other friends agreed with her with the nods of their heads.

Feeling somewhat defeated, Bola turned to Olúfúnmi with pursed lips and drooped eyelids. "Am I not your best friend?" she asked as more of a plea than a question. "You know that I like you most and I know you like me the most, right?" She twisted her body toward Bíọlá, rolled her eyes and did a mschew hissing at her.

Before Olúfúnmi had a chance to respond, Bíọlá interjected with her own mschew hissing from the corner teeth, drawing in more air for competitive elongation. She then planted herself in front of Olúfúnmi, intentionally blocking Bola off from view. "Fúnmi, you remember that this girl used to say bad things about you and your Màmá? She used to call you a spoiled rotten girl. Remember? And that your Màmá —"

Olúfúnmi raised her hand up to cut Bíọlá off. "We don't need to fight … Let's not argue," she pleaded in a soft voice. "We're all friends. You're all my best friends. I like all of you the same," teeth exposed, lips curled up and eyes gleaming, she coaxed.

After a brief awkward silence, "Let's play the *Tente* game and show the boys that we're not fighting," Olúfúnmi suggested and rolled her eyes at the group of boys who were part of Olúfúnmi's clique. They had been snickering throughout the feud between Bíọlá and Bola. Olúfúnmi started the handclapping in rhythm with foot-tapping on the dusty playground. The girls divided into two groups and lined up behind Olúfúnmi and Bola who had selected herself as the leader of the opposing group. Bíọlá placed herself behind Olúfúnmi. *"Tente…tente…tente…ìwo…ìwo…ìwo kẹ̀,"* they sang at each round. Some of the boys decided to help keep the scores of the *tente* while others occupied their time chasing after and kicking a thick rubber ball, targeting a post between two parallel trees hemming the bush.

On the day of coronation, Olúróunbí was given horses to transport her and daughter to the market every day. Her wardrobe and that of Olúfúnmi had transformed from tattered *Ankara* cotton print to silky thread handwoven *aṣọ-òkè* of the best quality by the best weaver. More children of Ìlúgidi had started competing to befriend Olúfúnmi, and more eligible men vied for Olúróunbí's attention.

On the other hand, Bàbá Ayọ̀'s negative feelings for Olúróunbí rose to a higher level, bordering on lethal hatred. He had forbidden her and Olúfúnmi from entering his compound despite entreaties from Ọba Ìlúgidi and other well-meaning members of the community. He maintained his decision and forbade his wife and other family members from interacting with them.

Chapter Twelve

ÌPADÀ DÉ ÌRÓKÒ - THE RETURN OF ÌRÓKÒ

Amid all the newly found success, Olúróunbí had forgotten all about the Ìrókò tree and the covenant she made with it. The seventh moon came and went without Olúróunbí thinking about the promise. On the first day of the eighth moon, the town was awoken by a terrible land tremor. The vibration beneath their sleeping mats, beds, and under their feet made them scurry in a panic, bumping into walls, trees, and one another like drunkards. "What is the matter? What's the matter?" they shouted.

Then suddenly, a deafening voice erupted from the earth, throwing the people into further confusion and fright.

"O-O-O-O-Olúúúú-ro-unbí-í-í!"

"O-O-O-O-Olúúúú-ro-unbí-í-í!"

"O-O-O-O-Olúúúú-ro-unbí-í-í!"

After a while, the townsfolk recognized the unmistakable voice of the Ìrókò tree even in its rare thunderous roar. They also recognized Olúróunbí's name and wondered why she was being summoned by the Ìrókò tree.

"O-O-O-O-Olúúúú-ro-unbíííííí!"!" The roaring voice and the land tremors continued until the town's elders had led Olúróunbí and the townsfolk who had all gathered at the town square to the foot of the tree.

The most superior of the elders stepped forward and started reciting the praise names and invocation of the Ìrókò tree spirit. When the elder beheld the tree gently swaying from left to right, he was encouraged and continued placating it for a while longer. Then, he extended his hands in its direction. "Oh, great king of the woods! King of all trees! What have we done to displease you this morning that you woke us up with such anger?"

Ìrókò replied, "You mortals! You humans! You are ungrateful! You always break your covenant. Olúróunbí—Olúróunbí entered into a covenant with me eight moons ago." The earth started trembling again as the Ìrókò tree spoke. "I gave her all that she asked for. I fulfilled my end of the covenant. I made her rich—richer than any person in this land. But she is ungrateful!"

At that moment, all eyes turned toward Olúróunbí. Olúróunbí's sunken shoulders quivered. She felt the familiar sting of tears welling up in her eyes which quickly made their way down her face. She did not bother to wipe them off, even though she had been cognizant of everyone's stares.

The elderly man approached Olúróunbí. "Is it true that you entered into an agreement with the great Ìrókò tree and you have not fulfilled your end of it?" he asked gently.

"Yes, Bàbá, but—" Sobbing, Olúróunbí's words choked in her throat. "But Bàbá, I can't give up my only child for sacrifice! Please, Bàbá, intercede on my behalf. Please, help me beg the great Ìrókò spirit to spare my only child."

The elder man turned toward the Ìrókò tree again and did as Olúróunbí requested. Others joined in the plea, but the Ìrókò tree was adamant in its refusal. As more and more people gathered around the great tree and begged it to spare the poor child, the Ìrókò tree began to lose its patience.

"Humans! Mortals!" it called out angrily. "You are fond of retracting your promises, even to God, *Elédùmarè*, but I shall not allow it this time. If you do not present me with my sacrifice, I shall cause the earth to swallow all of you this moment!"

On hearing this, the crowd turned on Olúróunbí, shouting their disapproval of her disloyalty to her honor and gesturing that she must release her daughter for the sacrificial presentation. Olúróunbí had no choice, she had to give up Olúfúnmi.

Chapter Thirteen
ÀLÁFÍÀ ÌYANU - MIRACULOUS RECOVERY

Nearby, a grey-haired man in a three-piece *agbádá* (*Men's flowy garment over top and bottom)* with matching *fìlà (hat)*, bent over, examining some roots before plucking them, and heard a deafening cry of a male human being. He recognized it as the sound of imminent death. He sprang upright and sprinted in the direction of the sound, leaving behind his bamboo woven basket, a hoe, a cutlass, and a knife. He raced through the forest like a panther, his grey hair was not congruent with the agility of his body. As he ran, words spilled out of his mouth. "By Your Name and Power, nothing can cause harm in the earth or above without Your Knowledge. You are All-Hearing and The All-Knowing. Please, protect me." in an auto-mode, he continued the scriptural recitation that he had committed to memory from childhood, "With Your permission, I invoke your Power to avert calamity and catastrophe from my path and anyone who seem to be in distress, Oh! Most Powerful *Adániwáyé* Creator of the universe and all that is within it."

Then, he sighted a very long snake slithering on top of an unmoving body stretched flat on the ground. The vertical snake was almost twice the length of the human. The grey-haired man slowed down, paused, and stared at the duo. He continued chanting the same mantra repeatedly. The snake uncurled the rest of its long body, giving the grey-haired man a chance to get a good look at it. He observed that it was, at least three times the length of the man spread on the ground. It then slithered off him. Pausing momentarily, it turned its head and glanced in the direction of the chanting voice. It stood on its belly, bringing it to eye-level with the man, regarding him. It paused again as if listening to the chant and contemplating its next move. Then, within a split second, it hacked up some lethal sputum and sent it flying towards the man standing feet away from it. The man, without breaking the prayer recital, stretched out his right arm and blocked the arsenal with his bare hand. He redirected fluid onto the ground. The snake issued a series of hisses, turned around and decided to take off at the speed of lightning into the denser part of the forest.

The grey-haired man, known as Bàbá Eléwé, hurried towards the lifeless-looking body on the ground. He continued to recite his prayers as he placed two fingers on the man's neck. He frowned, picked up his hand, pressed two fingers on his wrist, brought an ear to his chest, and listened intensely for a moment. He jerked up, quickly pushed his hands underneath the stiffening body and picked him up with a grunt. He wrapped one of the man's arms around his own neck, leaving the other one dangling on his side. Bàbá Eléwé hurriedly retrieved from pocket of his *bùbá* tunic some leaves called *Egbé*, He tucked a handful into the corners of his mouth, chewed them up and started reciting another set of prayers invoking the power given to the fastest terrestrial bird that enabled it to cover long distance within the twinkle of an eye to working for him this moment. Bàbá Eléwé had used this method of flight a few times before when he was in danger and it worked. In an instant, both men became weightless, disappeared from the farmland, and reappeared inside Bàbá Eléwé's fence erected with *màrìwò-ọpẹ* (palm tree fronds). The palm tree fronds were woven into many intricate layers and erected with bamboo sticks pillars. Bàbá Eléwé and the man landed aground. Still supporting him, Bàbá Eléwé helped him to one of his healing chambers and laid him on a cot alongside a wall. He could feel the lifeless body burning hot through his clothing. Before he took out a cow's horn suctioning instrument, he quickly removed his knee-length *agbádá* and bùbá proceeded to suction body fluids from the sites of the snake bites. The pressure of the procedure brought out a heart-wrenching sound from the man that left Bàbá Eléwé, who was accustomed to sounds of pain and suffering from ailing clients, unnerved.

Bàbá Eléwé picked up one of several cow's horns of varied sizes displayed on *pẹpẹ* (high shelf), dipped it into a sanitizing solution, attached a suctioning pump to the tip of the narrow end, placed the wide end to the sight of the first snake bite and proceeded to draw out the blood. With the first draw, Ayò howled so loud, nearby birds took flight and Bàbá Eléwé's wife who did not know that her husband had returned from his journey to the forests, rushed into the healing chamber in panic. Bàbá Eléwé turned towards the entrance and waved his greetings to her. Returning the greetings with a quick knee courtesy, she entered and proceeded to assist him.

"He was bitten by a strange and I believe a foreign snake near the forest where I was gathering herbs from. He was almost dead when I found him and the snake," Bàbá Eléwé explained as he worked quickly on the wounds.

"*Ennnn!*" she exclaimed, her eyes widened and lit up simultaneously.

"The snake was about to strike him again when I arrived and was distracted by my voice."

"*Eyah!* Thank God! The prayers, right?"

"You know it. It works all the time. We're favored *ooo*, my dear wife."

The man trembled vigorously and groaned with subsequent draws from the horn. The healer worked very fast with trained precision. He collected some leaves that his wife had retrieved from a large calabash bowl and rubbed them in between his palms. He squeezed drops of the extracted liquid onto the sites of Màmá Black Mamba's bites and placed the mashed leaves on top of the wounds. Bàbá Eléwé pointed to a cupboard on the other end of the chamber, his wife hurried to it, reached inside, brought out a cup, and dipped it into a pot of warm *àgbo ibà* (a medicinal herbal mixture containing Kigelia Africana, Nauclea Latifolia-Linn). He forced half a cupful of the àgbo down his patient's throat to reduce the fever and work as anti-virus and anti-bacteria on his body. After that, Bàbá Eléwé held the man's head in his hands and commenced another recitation for the sparing of his life and the restoration of his health. Upon completion of the first treatment, the man fell into a deep sleep. Bàbá Eléwé retired to his house where his meal was awaiting his return. During his meal, he narrated the fuller version of his eventful day to his wife. "You might as well include our new patient's meals in your daily cooking. As I see it, I think it will take a while for him to heal," he requested.

"Of course, my dear, ọkọ mi, *Olówó orí mi* (my husband, the payer of my dowry," endorsed Bàbá Eléwé's good-natured wife, pleasantly.

Meanwhile, the man did not wake up throughout the day, the following day, or several days after. He had fallen into a coma, which lasted several months to the surprise of the healer.

The day that he regained consciousness, Bàbá Eléwé slaughtered a ram in celebration and shared it among the villages as "a demonstration of gratitude to God, the Giver, and Restorer of life," he announced to the villagers.

Several moons had come and retired. The recovering patient had been drinking various herbal mixtures to heal the snake bite wounds, purify his blood from the toxins, and restore his memory. A broad grin spread across Bàbá Eléwé's face as he examined the locations of the snake bites on his legs. He nodded approvingly. "The Creator is benevolent. He has done good by you, young man," he declared.

"What magical power did you use to bring me back to life in the first place, Bàbá?" the man asked, brows furrowed.

"It's not a magical power, my son. It's a divine gift from the Creator. He gives it to whomsoever He wishes." Bàbá Eléwé smiled broadly. "We are just servants on errands to deliver His missions to His creations for one reason or another. It is He and only He who knows the reason why your life is restored and persevered. I'm just fortunate to be the vessel used to carry out His Plan for you. You have a great purpose to fulfill; otherwise, you should have died immediately. The snake that bit you is one of the deadliest and fastest snakes to kill humans and prey."

Hmmmmm. the man nodded, reflecting on the words of his savior. *God's emissary sent to save my life.*

"What am I going to be calling you pending the return of your memory? I can't just continue to call you young man all the time, can I?" Bàbá Eléwé chuckled. "There are numerous young men in this village, you know?" He tilted his head sideways in a thinking gesture and then announced, "I will call you Ọgbẹ́ni for now until you remember your name." He smiled at the newly named Ọgbẹ́ni, who smiled back at his benefactor.

At that moment, the man's brows wrinkled up, and a cloud of worries sailed onto his face. He strained his mind, trying to remember who he was. He knew he was presently alive and recuperating from snake bites according to the healer tending to him. He remembered everything Bàbá Eléwé told him, but he had no recollection of his existence prior to that. Bàbá Eléwé told him that he had been in a nine-moon slumber. He could not even recall if he dreamt or not during the long repose. No matter how many times or how hard he tried, he always drew a complete blank as if he had not existed before he had been saved. He frowned so hard until his head started aching. Once again, he decided to let it rest for the time being and continued taking the remedy Bàbá Eléwé gave him daily.

Bàbá Eléwé had become a teacher to the man during his healing time at his house. The man thought himself to be a learned person, however, he realized that he had much to learn in the world. Even though he had acquired so much knowledge about the herbs and roots from his father, the elders in the town, and several healers in the surrounding areas, it did not keep him from opening his mind's eyes to the world and how he was miraculously saved. He had developed a renewed thirst for knowledge. He asked endless questions from his new teacher and savior who seemed to be enjoying teaching as much as he was learning.

The student and the teacher engaged in discussions about the Order of Creation and the distribution of the earth's provisions. Bàbá Eléwé narrated to him how the first man and his female companion were charged with procreation to fill the earth.

He told him how the Creator had commanded all the progeny to descend from the back of this humongous man and then displayed before him and his wife what was brought forth from the man. He and his wife saw all the children that would come from them. Even though their skin color was of the darkest shade, the site of their posterity was of various colors, shades, and features, just as the earth from which they were created were of various colors, textures, and characteristics.

"Hmm, so that's why people come in different shades and colors."

"Yes, my son. And that's why some people are tough and feisty, and some are gentle and easy going. Some of the people who get very angry are made from volcanic matter, while those who are calm in nature are from the riverbank sand. Tough, rugged people are made with substance from rocky areas, such as mountains and hills."

"Amazing!" the man nodded repeatedly, contemplating the subject matter and applying the theory to some of the people he had encountered at Bàbá Eléwé's dwelling in Abàtà village. Being a highly respected elder in the community, a lot of family and relational feuds were brought to him for resolution as a mediator. His teacher usually invited him to such meetings and often sought his counsel on the matters at hand. Lately, the now almost fully healed man had been experiencing a feeling like a door somewhere in the recess of his mind was trying to unlock itself. Something was telling him that he knew people who fit into those categories. Whenever he encountered aggressive parties during the reconciliations, he found himself feeling agitated. He would recognize their texture being from the volcano regions of the earth. Bàbá Eléwé predicted that he must have been born by people of the calm riverside sand. He explained that such people are wise, confident, and calm. Musing over the diverse nature of mankind, the man traveled deep inside himself, trying to grapple with the nagging feeling that had been disturbing him in the last few days. *I feel like I knew a woman who must have been created with fine sands from a sacred and serene part of the earth.* As he thought about this, suddenly, he experienced a painful thud in his chest as if somebody had hit him with a sledgehammer.

During one of the arbitrations that Bàbá Eléwé was asked to preside over, a party of six men arrived at his compound. The dispute was over a piece of land in a nearby pastoral village. They sat on wooden carved benches placed under the luscious leafy Igi Ọdàn tree. The man was formally introduced as Ọgbẹ́ni. Ọgbẹ́ni recognized three of the men because they often came to purchase herbal mixtures from Bàbá Eléwé. He did not recognize the other three men because he had never seen them since he had been living in Abàtà village. After exchanging greetings and pleasantries, the meeting commenced. As it progressed, Ọgbẹ́ni observed that one of the unknown men kept staring at him. At the end of the meeting, Ọgbẹ́ni observed the men whispering while peering at him and nodding intermittently. He became curious and concerned at the same time. He contemplated interrogating them about it, but they hurried away before he got a chance to do so. He shrugged it off after a while and forgot all about it.

Chapter Fourteen

ỌGBẸ́NI TI FARASIN – THE DISAPPEARANCE OF ỌGBẸ́NI

Two houses had been chosen many generations ago as the rotational custodians and protectors of the sovereignty of the seven circular towns and villages, which included Ìlúgidi and Kẹ́lẹ́gbẹ́ - Mẹgbẹ́ shortened to Kẹ́lẹ́gbẹ́ town. No one knew when the agreement was made stipulating that the first grandson of the first son of a current head of the family of the largest twin towns would be installed as the custodian and protector of their sovereignty. The position was the most revered in this union's land mass, except for the *ọba* (kings). Bàbá Ayọ̀, being the current head of the Àjàní household, had been eagerly expecting his son, Ayọ̀, since his nineteenth birthday, to get married and give birth to a son before his rival, Bámijí Àjàkayé did.

Eventually, Ayọ̀ gave birth to Olúfúnmi. Incidentally, his rival Bámijí Àjàkayé from Kẹ́lẹ́gbẹ́ town also gave birth to a female as his first child, followed quickly by another daughter within eighteen moons. Feeling highly pressured, he took a second wife in the hopes that the second wife would give him a son. She gave birth to females, Táíwò, Kẹ́hìndé, and Ìdòwú within a period of three years. *Wàhálà ré o*, Bàbá Bámijí thought, furious with his son. "What's your problem?" he lashed out at his one day. "Don't you have any sons in your loin? Your sister has all boys! Four sons to be exact and not a single daughter, *hennn.*" *Unfortunately, by default, none of them are eligible to carry the sovereignty of the seven lands,* he fumed inside.

The pressure was tremendous on the two first sons of the rivaling twin towns. However, Ayọ̀ did not share the ambition as did his counterpart from Kẹ́lẹ́gbẹ́. Annually, they engaged in warfare exercise and training. This event had a dual purpose: to be prepared to defend the union and to gauge their respective skills in a competitive way.

In the last six years, Bámijí Àjàkayé led the Kẹ́lẹ́gbẹ́ young warriors in a friendly non-fatal warfare scrimmage against the Ìlúgidi warriors led by Ayọ̀. Ìlúgidi warriors had more victories— five to one—than Kẹ́lẹ́gbẹ́ town to the displeasure of Ọba Kẹ́lẹ́gbẹ́ and their patriarchal leaders. When the people of Kẹ́lẹ́gbẹ́ heard that Ayọ̀ Àjàní's wife, Olúróunbí gave birth to a female baby, they jubilated. They had renewed hope that Bámijí had been given another chance to beat Ayọ̀ at producing an heir to the highly coveted crown.

Disappointed and unhappy, Bámijí blamed his two wives for the failure to have a son and often threatened them with marrying a third wife. Even though he was not supposed to, Bàbá Bámijí had disclosed to his son the secret that he stood a chance to be the father of the next Ọba (King) of the seven united towns and villages if his opponent at Ìlúgidi, Ayọ̀ Àjàní failed to produce a male child. Therefore, when the Bámijí and his father heard about Ayọ̀'s death and the disappearance of his body, they felt a sense of relief and renewed hope for a chance to direct the chieftaincy to their town.

The two wives of Bámijí conceived again, four months apart. They engaged in a fierce rivalry over their husband's attention, favors, and love. Each strived to be the first to produce a male child to carry on his lineage, as most African men desired. They were not aware that there was more to Bámijí's interest in having a son than the usual machismo value of society. They were not privy to the knowledge. The expectant mothers had to drink some herbal leaves and root cocktail mixture prescribed by the best herbal doctors in Kẹ́lẹ́gbẹ̀. The herbs were known to aid in ensuring that the gender of the fetus was male. The wives drank them with religious tenacity.

Bámijí's wives were in their second and third trimester when his childhood friend from a village, called Abàtà, invited him along as a character witness in a land dispute. Abàtà was a full day's journey from Kẹ́lẹ́gbẹ́ on foot. Bámijí did not mind the sacrifice because his friend had also stood by him on several occasions throughout their friendship. When they presented at the arbitration meeting, Bámijí was shocked to find Ayọ̀ Àjàní there. He was seated beside the elder arbitrator known as Bàbá Eléwé. As Bámijí made a gesture to greet his adversary, he noticed that there was no sign of recognition on Ayọ̀'s face. He greeted him casually as if they were meeting for the first time while he greeted the other group with familiarity. Bámijí was confused but careful. He maintained his composure but continued to examine him from a distance. A thought ran through his mind—that the man who was introduced to the party as Ọgbẹ́ni was not Ayọ̀ but his twin from God. Yorùbá people generally believe that God created every person in a pair of the same gender. Bámijí's second thought was that Ọgbẹ́ni must be the *òkúdàáyà* of Ayọ̀. Some believed that a person who died an untimely tragic death would not report to God in Heaven (O*lorun*) but would migrate instead to another place to live out the rest of his or her life there until old age. In either case, Bámijí was not taking chances by identifying himself to this Ọgbẹ́ni. He decided to wait till after the meeting to inquire from his friend. As soon as the meeting ended, Bámijí pulled his friend aside. "Who is that man called Ọ̀gbẹ́ni and what's his story?" he asked, almost breathlessly.

Bámijí's friend turned and pointed at Ayọ̀ with the protrusion of his lips. "You mean Bàbá Eléwé's visiting student?"

"Visiting student?" Bámijí asked, more perturbed.

"Yes."

"Visiting student?" he repeated. "Visiting from where? Where did he come from?"

"No one knows where he came from. Even he doesn't know where he came from."

"All we know is that he was bitten by a snake. Bàbá Eléwé found him almost dead, brought him home, and healed him."

Bámijí's eyes widened, his heart race stepped up a notch, and his voice became somewhat raspy. "Do you know how long ago it happened?" he pressed further.

"Hmm." He scratched his head and rolled his eyes upward. "It's been a while. He was unconscious but alive for about a year; then he couldn't walk for many moons," he narrated.

Bámijí noticed that Ayọ̀ had started toward them; he grabbed his friend by the arm and walked briskly in the opposite direction. "Let's go. We'll continue this discussion at your house."

As soon as they reached the house, Bámijí chronicled Ayọ̀'s story to his friend and outlined a plan that he called extremely necessary and that would require his assistance and cooperation.

Since everyone believed that Ayọ̀'s child, Olúfúnmi, could never become the custodian and protector of the sovereignty of the two towns, they decided to prevent the return of Ayọ̀ to his hometown. They knew that if he were to return to his family, then he stood a chance of having a son, after all. So, they plotted and kidnapped Ayọ̀ from Bàbá Eléwé of *abúlé Àbàtà* village before the herbal memory therapy worked on him. They knew that it was a matter of time before the herbs worked on Ayọ̀. They planned to hold him captive in an undisclosed location in a forest near Abàtà village. After concluding on this plan with his friend, Bámijí traveled back on borrowed horseback to inform his father. The horse ride back cut the journey in half. As soon as he arrived in the town of Kẹ́lẹ́gbẹ́—Mẹgbẹ́, Bámijí summoned himself to a private counsel with his father who demonstrated delight at the prospect. Rubbing his palms against each other, humming amusing hymn, Bàbá Bámijí finally spoke, "This is a good development." He looked at his son with penetrating eyes, "We must make sure Ayọ̀ is not hurt. We cannot have his blood on our hands, otherwise, we're doomed for generations." Bàbá Bámijí and Bámijí sketched the plan and went over it several times to ensure the successful kidnapping and imprisonment of Ayọ̀ in a remote secret dwelling in the Agijùn Forest without shedding his blood or killing him. Bámijí was to set out the following day for Abàtà village to carry out the scheme.

Chapter Fifteen
OJÓ PÉ – THE ARRIVAL OF THE DAY

Back in the earthquake-riddled town of Ilugidi, an elderly man put up his hands to silence the crowd, then stood before Olúróunbí. "If that is what you promised to give the Ìrókò tree in exchange for the wealth it granted you, you must fulfill your end of the bargain," he declared gently. An emissary was immediately dispatched to go and fetch Olúróunbí's only child, Olúfúnmi. When they arrived, she was in a daze from the clamor and earth tremor that had occurred a short time ago. She tried to piece together bits and pieces of information from the townsfolk about her mother's promise to Ìrókò. Her name was mentioned, and she was carried by two strong men to Ìdí Ìrókò. Olúfúnmi had not resisted. The loud pounding in her chest drowned out the clatter of a thousand voices all speaking at once.

Olúfúnmi sought out and spotted her mother even before they reached Ìdí Ìrókò. She saw her being restrained by several women. As she was carried close enough, her mother lurched forward and grabbed for her. Some of the women pulled her away and held her firmly in place.

Suddenly, Olúfúnmi felt herself snap out of the stupor and made for her mother. Her escape attempt was futile because the town's head *Babaláwo*, reciting incantations, slapped his hand against Olúfúnmi's chest, and she felt her body go limp. She lost the ability to resist. Her muscles had suddenly turned to jelly, even though she was aware of everything around her. She could not talk, scream, or run. She could see the knowing expression on people's faces, including her mother's. They knew what the head of the council of elders did. They knew he had put the tranquilizer spell on her. She had heard stories of how the tranquilizer had been used to abduct children and adults by wicked people who used them for money-making rituals. She realized that she was facing a similar fate. The difference between her and those that had been abducted was that her mother and the townspeople offered her as a sacrifice.

When they arrived, bearing the young *ọmọ-pupa-apọ́n-bí-epo* —skin-as-red-as-palm-oil—child in their arms, Olúróunbí darted to snatch her away. But the women, expecting such a maternal act, moved swiftly out of her reach. She jumped and pedaled her feet, but her body was prevented from reaching her destination. She was no match for the women holding on to her. She eventually crumpled onto their bosoms. She was oblivious of the tears and snot that welled down her face onto her blouse.

"I am begging you, great Ìrókò tree spirit, please, spare my child; she is my one and only child. Please."

"You must fulfill your promise, Olúróunbí. You knew she was your only child when you promised her as a sacrifice to me. I want the child whose skin is as red as palm oil. Olúróunbí's promise must be fulfilled."

As she begged the Ìrókò tree, the womenfolk joined her in begging. The men also joined in.

The townsfolk chorused, "Oh great Ìrókò tree, please spare our child, Olúfúnmi *ọmọ-pupa-apọ́n-bí-epo*."

"Ìrókò tree, take back your riches. I don't want to be the richest person in the land. All I want now is my child, Olúfúnmi *ọmọ-pupa-apọ́n-bí-epo*."

Suddenly, a thunderous sound came forth. "Mortals! Bring forth my request or else."

"Ìrókò, please forgive me and spare my child. Take back all that you've given me and let me be as I was before." She turned to the elder man. "Bàbá, please, help me appease the Ìrókò spirit."

As the elder opened his mouth to speak, the earth trembled again and this time, the earth opened in various places, and long branches of roots crawled out like snakes and curled around the feet of the townsfolk. The force of the roots' grip on the people's feet sent them into a renewed panic.

"If you do not bring me Olúfúnmi, you shall cease to exist above the earth!" Ìrókò issued fiercely.

"Give Ìrókò its request, now!" shouted the townsfolk. "It was Olúróunbí who promised Ìrókò her child, not us. We can't pay for her sin *ooo*."

Olúfúnmi was hastily carried to the foot of the tree and placed with her back against the trunk.

Olúróunbí took advantage and ran towards Ìrókò, grabbed her daughter and rushed away from it. She tried to escape through the crowd but was intercepted by the muscular guards. She wrestled with all might to hold on to her daughter. However, she was no match for them. They forcefully peeled Olúfúnmi from her mother's bosom and took back to the tree.

An opening like an elevator door appeared in the trunk of the tree, and Olúfúnmi was sucked in like a vacuum cleaner and disappeared through it.

The spectators gasped in horror to see the Ìrókò tree swallow Olúfúnmi right before their eyes. Olúróunbí's wailing intensified. She continued struggling to break free from the women's hold to retrieve her daughter, but it was no use. Olúfúnmi was gone. The womenfolk broke out in a moaning song:

Oníká-lukú jẹ̀jẹ́ ewúrẹ̀, ewúrẹ̀, ewúrẹ̀
(Everyone promised a goat)
Oníká-lukú jẹ̀jẹ́ àgùntàn, àgùntàn gbọ̀lọ̀jọ̀
Everyone promised ram, a robust ram)
Olúróunbí jẹ̀jẹ́ ọmọ rẹ̀, ọmọ-apọ́n-bí-epo
(Olúróunbí promised her child, child-as-red-as-palm-oil)
Olúróunbí o, jon-jon, Ìrókò jon-jon
Olúróunbí oh jon-jon, Ìrókò jon-jon

As they sang and watched the tree that had swallowed Olúfúnmi, the hole through which she had disappeared opened again. Olúfúnmi was seen being led away through a well-lit corridor that stretched endlessly for miles. She stretched out one arm toward them, calling, "Màmá mi! Màmá mi *ooo*! Save me! Save me, Maamaa mi *ooo*."

Olúróunbí, with determination and revived vigor, strove to break free from the women who held her down. Then the opening closed again. The last sound they heard from within the Ìrókò tree was, "Olúfúnmi, you will take your place as the princess of the woods among your peers."

After a while, the womenfolk forcefully led Olúróunbí away from the forest while whispering consoling words into her ears. She wanted to save her only child, her joy, her happiness. Fighting and struggling fiercely to wrench herself from the grips of the women, she screamed, wailed, sobbed, and cursed at Ìrókò, the elders, herself, and death, who had taken her husband away in the first place. From deep in her guts, she cried out, making even her enemies feel pity for her, "*Ẹjọ̀,* all I want is my child, my red-as-palm-oil child, Olúfúnmi *Ọmọ-pupa-apọ́n-bí-epo.* I don't want to be rich anymore. Ìrókò! *Jọ̀wọ́, bámi gbé ọmọ mi!* Give me back my child! I don't want to be *Ìyálọ́jà (Market Leader).* I don't want to be the richest woman in Ìlúgidi. I just want my child back." Olúróunbí continued to wail as she was dragged along toward her house. *Yeeee!* Ìrókò has devoured my only child, *mogbé ooo.* My life is completely ruined."

"That will teach you a lesson, henceforth, not to make promises that you cannot fulfill."

Ìrókò's voice was heard again through the tree trunk. "Next time, you will not make covenants flippantly that you do not intend to keep. This is a lesson for mankind." His voice faded away into the recess of the Ìrókò tree.

Chapter Sixteen
ÈKÓ -LAGOS, NIGERIA
STILL 1975

Alhaji Ọlọ́mọwẹ́wẹ́ paused, his eyes sweeping from right to left over the upturned heads popping eyes, and downward smiley face quivering lips. He observed that tears were crawling down the faces of some of the younger girls and boys, while the older ones forced theirs to remain locked in. However, the faces of all the children and the majority of the adults mirrored varying degrees of emotional zigzag during the narration. Alhaji smiled, making sure he had eye contact with every one of his audience, even if for a fleeting moment. "Well, the evening is far spent. We have to stop here for tonight," he announced. As expected, a combination of growls and hisses of protest sounded out from the audience on the mat before him. Alhaji raised his eyes towards the dark twinkling sky and then at the gold-plated Seiko watch on his wrist. In obedience to Alhaji's cues, the adults rose from their chairs, one after the other and started to shuffle their way through the still seated children scattered on the multi-colored multi-texture mats.

The fidgety seven-year-old boy, Kúnlé, nicknamed *Ara-ò-balẹ̀; o*lórí àrùn (hyperactivity is a supreme malady) raised one hand up while waving the other one frantically at Alhaji, "please … please … please, sir, I have a question, sir," he begged. "Just one question, sir."

Alhaji pointed a permission-granting index finger at him. "Alright, Kúnlé, go ahead. What's your question?" he asked.

His grateful smile made Alhaji feel warm inside. He smiled back at Kúnlé. Alhaji liked him. He exuded good-natured personality, even with the meanness towards him from some of the children and adults who insisted on tagging *Ara-ò-balẹ̀* at the end of his first name as if he caused hyperactive and impulsive symptoms onto himself. Alhaji could understand that children could be mean because they did not know better, but he refused to excuse adults who should be more sensitive to the feelings of others, especially children. He had addressed the senseless behaviors of some of the erring adults more than necessary. Kúnlé loved to run errands for anyone who needed him to.

"Is Olúfúnmi gone inside Ìrókò tree forever? Is she gone forever? will she not see her mother ever again? did Ìrókò tree …"

Alhaji interrupted Kúnlé with the gesture of his hand. "My dear Kúnlé, I thought you said you have only one question, not ten," chuckled Alhaji infecting others in the audience. "Anyway, we're not going to be able to know that tonight," he repeated.

Alhaji granted permission to one of the boys in the clique that was in constant rivalry with Làbákẹ́. The boy triumphantly jumped to feet and with an air of importance, answered, "Did Olúróunbí give Ìrókò tree all the money back? And did she become poor again? Did Ọba Ìlúgidi banish her from the town because she caused the earthquake that destroyed the town?" He glanced over at Làbákẹ́, his eyes gleaming with pride, then at his group members who signaled several thumbs-up at him. Alhaji could not help the tickle in his throat. He succumbed to chuckles. "Very good questions but like I said earlier, we won't know until we hear the rest of the story next time. No more questions tonight," he announced.

Alhaji, still seated, winked at the standing adults who nodded their acquiescence for him to proceed with the next part of the story, continued, "Before we disperse, as usual, I also have a few questions for you, my children, to ponder and reflect on," Alhaji announced. "So, put on your thinking caps."

The children roared their affirmative response, as usual.

"What are the moral lessons of this story? Who would like to go first?"

Làbákẹ́'s hand was the first among several hands that flew up, waving, "me! me! me! ..." repeatedly.

Alhaji granted permission to speak to his young audience; and one after another, they provided various answers. One child stated, "When we make a promise, we must fulfill it, sir." Another mentioned that "Mothers must not give their children to a tree." Làbákẹ́ contributed that "We should not be wicked like Bàbá Ayọ̀." One girl encouraged learning about "the herbs in the bush so we can help sick people from snake bites."

In consideration of time and those who had been on their feet since the interactive adjournment session, Alhaji Ọlọ́mọwẹ́wẹ́ pleaded to end the evening with a promise to tell them the rest of the story at the next opportune time, "With the prayer that God should preserve our lives and health."

THE PAUSE

215

ÌDÚPẸ́ - DEDICATION

My gratitude is offered to the Almighty Creator of the universe and all that is in it, The Supreme God of all.

This book is dedicated to my family, starting with my late father, Chief Imam Sheikh Prince Muritala (Murtadha) Àkànbí Akóredé, who was a great storyteller among his many talents and gifts; and to his partner in birthing me into this world, my sweet superwoman, Alhaja Chief Hassanat Táíwò Àkànkẹ́ Akóredé-Balógun, who always puts her children first after God and The Prophet (SAW).

I am grateful for the tremendous support and immeasurable love from my children, Aisha &, Ibraheem Babájídé Ọ̀sányìn, their son, Abdul-Raheem Hakeem Babátúndé Ọ̀sányìn, Rashidat Ọmọlọlá, Muhibat Ọlábòmí and Muhammed Folahanmi Ẹdúnjọbí-II "MJ". Their faith in God and belief in me gave me the confidence to hop on my rainbow to reach my star. Their tireless assistance in proofreading and editing greatly contributed to the successful completion of this work. The birth of my first grandson, Abdul-Raheem Hakeem Babátúndé Ọ̀sányìn, infused my life with unparalleled energy, joy, and enthusiasm to keep on working through the storm of book writing. As if the Universe knew what I needed next, its Lord sent me a wonderful companion in the person of Sheikh Uthman Musa Ọláìtán (Al-Ilori) to spice things up. His advent brought along much needed spousal support and unexpectedly a vast knowledge in farming, herbal medicine, nature, animals, the woods, healing, prevention, The Scripture, Yorùbá and Arabic languages, culture, customs, and traditions.

I also dedicate this book to each of my twenty siblings from both parents: the nuclear and extended members of Akóredé and the Alli-Balógun clan.

This is also in memory of many departed loved ones, among whom are my beloved father, Alhaji Muritala Akorede, my mother's twin brother, Mr. Hussain Kehinde Uthman, my father's sisters and brothers, my first husband, the Late Alhaji Abdul-

Hakeem Àjàó Adégbindin and my brother, Abdul-Hafeez Akóredé, and my friend's son, a beautiful young soul, Fuad "Muyiwa Matti. The late Hakeem Adébáyọ̀ who played a significant role in supporting my writing career in 1989 by paying off a publisher a large sum of money to retrieve my first manuscript from them after leaving Nigeria. I pray that you all rest in perfect peace and comfort in the bowel of mother earth.

I have been blessed to have so many God-sent kind people supporting me through thick and thin to keep me of sound mind and nourished body to see this day. It is impossible to list them all, but I ask you to be blessed for eternity. To mention a few, Alhaji Luqman Ìyàndá Akóredé, Prince Ayọ̀ & Adéníké Akóredé (Bàbá Zeenah), Alhaji Bashir & Mrs. Kafilat Akóredé-Bello, Fatima Akóredé-Ọdúnewu, Mrs. Kẹmi & Dr. Túnjí Aláúsá, Mr. & Mrs. O. J. Lawal, Sandra Jackson-Opoku, Asi Williams, Alhaji Shewu & Wanda Akóredé, My beautiful inspiring longtime friends, Hanan Wajid and Kitten "Kat" Grey, the Alli family of Alhaja Rafatu, Alhaji Salman Akóredé & family, Kafilat

Abdul-Majeed, Alhaja Fatimo Solomon, Alhaji & Alhaja Sàrùmí, Ahrif Sàrùmí, and all the Akóredés from Ògbómọ̀shọ́ and Abẹ̀òkúta. I am grateful to Mrs. Rashidat Kíkẹ́ and Ambassador Rafiu Bello for allowing me to use the west wing of their home for a solo writer's retreat. Mr. and Mrs. Kẹhìndé and Lọlá Alli were consistently supportive in so many ways. To Mrs. Jane Schelander, my English Literature professor at King Abdulaziz University in Jeddah, Saudi Arabia who helped me discover my writing skills when she shocked me in 1980 with a statement, "You write well, I will make a good writer out of you."

It's my pleasure to acknowledge the spiritual nurturing, love and support that the Nigerian-American Muslim communities in Houston, Texas (Ansar-Ud-Deen SW-Houston and the North America continent (ADSNA) under the leadership of The Worldwide Missioner, Chief Imam Abdur-Rahman Ọlánrenwájú Ahmad, Houston NASFAT, Masjid-ul Mumineen, and in Chicago area: Light of Islam (LOI) and Nigerian Islamic Association (NIA), University of Chicago Muslim Students

Association as well as in other parts of the United States, and Nigeria.

To everyone that I have mentioned and those that I could not mention, I pray that goodness and blessings come back around to you and yours.

ÌJẸ́Ẹ̀RÍ –
ACKNOWLEDGEMENT

First and foremost, I acknowledge the presence and manifestation of God in my life as The Controller and Discharger of my affairs. Then I acknowledge the support, contribution and hard work of the following people/entity to the successful completion of this project:

Súnkànmí Akínbóyè, my illustrator, who put up with my tough demands in portraying and giving visual to what was in my head onto his working material. He patiently drafted and re-drafted each artwork until I was satisfied.

Mrs. Reyhanat Títí and Dr. Tijani Mọ́gàjí along with Ismail Gbénga and Tósìn Alli-Balógun were instrumental in scouting for the right artist in Nigeria and overseeing the contract transaction on my behalf with Súnkànmí Akínbóyè.

Ms. Asi (Azeezat) Williams who refused to let me rest by insisting that I must continue to publish my work. My daughter, Mrs. Aisha Ọsányìn's confidence in my writing was demonstrated in her relentless encouragement and support. She encouraged participation in writers' groups, conferences, and workshops; and often paid applicable fees and charges.

My in-house proofreaders, editors and critiques, Ms. Rashidat, Muhibat, Aisha and Muhammed, who despite their respective busy lives, created time to help me do the necessary work. By and by, Mrs. Fadheelah Ọpẹ́yẹmí Ṣódípẹ̀-Ọ̀kánlàwọ́n came along, supported by her husband, Mr. Abdulaziz Ọ̀kánlàwọ́n, and provided a valuable contribution to proofreading and editing. In addition, Mrs. Fadheelah (thanks to her father, Alhaji Nurudeen Ṣódípẹ̀, a lecturer at the Federal College of Education, Abẹ́òkúta, Ògùn State who taught her the language) is responsible for the accenting and tone-marking of all the Yorùbá words and names in this book. Before discovering this gem, the world's nicest journalist in the United Kingdom Diaspora, Mr. Wale Hassan, had volunteered to carry out the task, in addition to his free blasting of my book on his Live Facebook show, 'ṢÉ Ẹ WÀ?' (Are you fine?).

I appreciate Tiffany Miller for creating the initial publishing roadmap of Olúróunbí's Promise and exposing me to the complex nuances of the creature called Publishing.

I acknowledge the exceptional peer critique of this book by the Houston Writers Guild, especially the constructive feedback from Alex Perry and Pat Daily which is part of the reason the story was expanded from less than 40 pages to 200 pages. The exposure into the writing and publishing industry gained as a member of the Houston Chapter Society of Children's Books Writers and Illustrators (SCBWI) has been outstandingly educative and inspiring.

My mother, Alhaja Hassanat Táíwò Akóredé-Balógun's 24/7 prayers and regular status checking-in, *"Ṣé oti ko ìwé yen tán? Ọlọrun ábá ẹṣẹ o,"* was evidently accepted and granted by God. *Alhamdulillah*, Glory be to God.

Even though he prefers to be an invisible support system, Alhaji Mr. O. J. Lawal demonstrated his endorsement of my creative and entrepreneurial aspiration by providing positive reinforcement and a jumpstart. *Jazaakunmullah Kheiran.*

My sincere gratitude also extends to those that I did not mention herein. God's Blessings on you and yours.

NÍPA OLÙKÒTÀN - ABOUT THE AUTHOR

Princess Sherifat Akóredé hails from the Láoyè Akóredé Dynasty of Ògbómọ̀shọ́, Ọ̀yọ́ State, Nigeria by way of her father who was a Nigerian diplomat and Chief Imam. She's the voiceover talent that translated the anthropology documentary, *Birth of the Princess*, adapted and co-produced by award-winning UCLA professor, Dr. Andrew Apter. Sherifat has published two timely journals in her tenure, "Religion, Politics, and Women: The Politics of Exclusion and Inclusion" and "Osama bin Laden and the Saudi Opposition," both presented for selection by Chicago State University. Her work has been published in the literary anthology, NOMMO, a project developed by the Organization of Black

American Culture. She is the author of *Olúróunbí's Promise*; and the soon to be released *Olúfúnmi Ọmọ Olúróunbí -The Accidental She-hero*, *Love on the Arabian Sand*, and *Tears of a Yorùbá Bride*. Princess Sherifat received her bachelor's degree in English literature and has two master's degrees from the University of Chicago. She is currently working as a licensed master social worker in the state of Texas and resides in the Houston area with her family.

NÍPA OLÙ YÀWÒRÁN - ABOUT THE ILLUSTRATOR

Súnkànmí Akínbóyè is a Nigeria-based Illustrator, specialized in comic books, graphic novels & concept art. He began working for Calabash magazine under Moses Ebong while studying art in Yaba College of Technology, Lagos.

Since then, he has worked with several clients such as YouNeek Studios Maryland, USA, publisher of the critically acclaimed E.X.O Graphic Novel featured on CNN Africa, Mashable, Forbes and BBC, Farafina Magazine, Onward Paper Mill, True Tarpan UK, FansConnectOnline Limited; the creators of the award-winning Afrinolly App, and CSED; publishers of the first ever Nigerian sports-themed Graphic Novel; Nigerian Golden Legends.